LAUGHING BOY,

who knew nothing of the white man, who had grown up worshipping the Indian gods, following the old familiar ways, mastering the traditional skills, and exulting in the physical freedom and code of values that were his birthright ...

SLIM GIRL,

who knew all too much about the white man; who had been turned by his schools and abuse into a person without a true culture, converted by his lust into a woman who dreamed of money and revenge; who saw in Laughing Boy the sole hope for her salvation . . .

BETWEEN THEM LOVE HAPPENED —WITH ITS JOY, ITS PAIN, AND ITS TRAGEDY . . .

"Lucid beauty, vital artistic imagination, and a clear, almost hypnotic style."

—*The New York Times*

SIGNET CLASSICS by American Authors

Laughing Boy

Oliver La Farge

A SIGNET CLASSIC

NEW AMERICAN LIBRARY

SIGNET, SIGNET CLASSIC, MENTOR, PLUME, MERIDIAN AND NAL
BOOKS *are published by New American Library,
1633 Broadway, New York, New York 10019*

FIRST SIGNET PRINTING, SEPTEMBER, 1971

12   13   14   15   16   17   18   19   20

PRINTED IN THE UNITED STATES OF AMERICA

FOREWORD

THIS book was written about a people who have now vanished, by a young man, now long gone, whom once I knew intimately. He was a young man composed of a mixture of elements; he was rather ferocious, romantic, and at the same time — so I have been told by competent judges — had the makings of a good scientist in him. The book sprang from a combination of vivid memory, the sad sense of saying farewell, and the knowledge acquired in writing a thesis as part of the requirements for a master's degree.

He believed, at the time he wrote the book, that he might never go to the American Southwest again, certainly would never again be free to soak himself in the Navajo Indians. Among them he had seen something that had moved him greatly and this was his way of recording it. As the young can do, he had made personal friendships, experienced moments of genuine contact among the Navajos, despite the barriers of language and culture, and these loopholes of insight were vastly widened by his studies.

Writing between 1926 and 1928 about what he had experienced some years earlier, romanticism made him feel that he should cast back in time to a less corrupted, purer era, so he chose 1915 as the date of his story. That was the year when the first automobile made it through Marsh Pass into Kayenta in the north Navajo country, an event that, to his mind, marked a turning point.

Once he got going, he gave little thought to the date and simply described what he had seen. Whether anybody like Laughing Boy or Slim Girl ever could exist I do not know; he thought they could. That somes within the heart and essence of fiction and there is no use debating it. The general scene, the appearance and behavior of those Indians, their dress, their camps, their games, their weapons, their land, were honorably set down as he had seen them. Even Laughing Boy's black mare was drawn from life.

For the writer and for the Navajos that was an age of innocence. By and large, the Navajos liked the way they were living, they felt secure, they enjoyed life, they knew how to have fun, they were wonderfully friendly. The beginning anthropologist who went among them could believe, as they did, that their general condition and mode of life, with all its hardships, simplicity, and riches, could continue indefinitely if only they were not interfered with. The collapse of that way of life began in 1933.

It was believed in the 1920's that there were 25,000 Navajos; the number was more likely somewhat over 40,000. There are now about 85,000, a powerful community equipped with a modern government and many other imporvements, treated with great respect by the Senators and Congressmen from the two states in which most of them reside. They are an unhappy people, sullen towards all others, unfriendly, harassed by drunkenness, their leaders at once arrogant and touchy. Still, here and there among them you can still find the beauty, the religion, the sense of fun, you can still attend a ceremony at which no one is drunk. In the space of thirty years, however, the wholeness has gone, the people described in *Laughing Boy*, complete to itself, is gone.

It would have completely staggered that beginning writer to learn that after all these years his book would still be selling. He did not expect it to sell at all. It would have staggered and gratified him enormously could he have known then, in his time of early struggle, the days of aching hope and profound self-doubt, that young readers would still be liking it thirty years later. But there is no way to reach back and tell him that, and it probably is better that he did the thing for itself, because he had to, and for no other reason. That leaves the gratification to me, his successor, who am much older and much more in need of encouragement.

SANTA FE, 1962   O. LA. F.

INTRODUCTORY NOTE
TO THE ORIGINAL EDITION

THIS book is a work of fiction. I have tried to be as true as I knew how to the general spirit of Navajo things, to customs and character, but all personages and incidents in the story are fictitious, as well as places. I have used some real place-names applied to imaginary places, or else have shifted them a hundred miles or so. There are about thirty thousand Navajos, most of whom have at least two descriptive names; it would be impossible, then, to invent names for all my characters and not hit upon some real ones. So I have frankly borrowed from names I have heard, or those listed by scientists. But neither whites nor Indians are real.

I have been as accurate as possible about ceremonies, rites, and customs. If occasionally I have taken liberties, I plead a writer's privilege. Any innovations I may have made are none the less true to the general pattern of Navajo ideas.

This story is meant neither to instruct nor to prove a point, but to amuse. It is not propaganda, nor an indictment of anything. The hostility with which certain of the characters in it view Americans and the American system is theirs, arising from the plot, and not the author's. The picture is frankly one-sided. It is also entirely possible.

O. LA F.

NEW ORLEANS, 1929

CHAPTER ONE

I

HE was riding the hundred miles from T'o Tlakai to Tsé Lani to attend a dance, or rather, for the horse-racing that would come afterwards. The sun was hot and his belly was empty, but life moved in rhythm with his pony loping steadily as an engine down the miles. He was lax in the saddle, leaning back, arm swinging the rope's end in time to the horse's lope. His new red headband was a bright colour among the embers of the sun-struck desert, undulating like a moving graph of the pony's lope, or the music of his song—

> *'Nashdui bik'é dinni, eya-a, eyo-o . . .*
> Wildcat's feet hurt, *eya-a, eyo-o . . .'*

Rope's end, shoulders, song, all moved together, and life flowed in one stream. He threw his head back to sing louder, and listened to the echo from the cliffs on his right. He was thinking about a bracelet he should make, with four smooth bars running together, and a turquoise in the middle—if he could get the silver. He wished he could work while riding; everything was so perfect then, like the prayers, *hozoji nashad,* travelling in beauty. His hands, his feet, his head, his insides all were *hozoji,* all were very much alive. He whooped and struck up the Magpie Song till the empty desert re-sounded—

> *'A-a-a-iné, a-a-a-iné,*
> *Ya-a-iné-ainé, ko-ya-ainê . . .'*

He was lean, slender, tall, and handsome, Laughing Boy, with a new cheap headband and a borrowed silver belt to make ragged clothes look fine.

At noon, having no money, he begged coffee from a trader at Chinlee and went on, treasuring his hunger because of the feasting to come. Now he began to meet Navajos of all ages, riding to the dance. The young men bunched together—a line of jingling bridles, dark, excited faces, flashing silver, turquoise, velveteen shirts, dirty, ragged overalls, a pair of plaid calico leggins, a pair of turkey-red ones. Some of them were heavy with jewelry; Horse Giver's Son wore over four hundred dollars in silver alone; most of them had more than Laughing Boy. They stopped to look at his bow-guard, which he himself had made.

'I am a good jeweller,' he said, elated; 'I make silver run like a song.'

'You should make a song about yourself,' they told him, 'and teach the burros to sing it.'

'Have you had any rain up by T'o Tlakai?'

'No, it is just like last year. It is the devil. The grass is all dried up and the sheep are dying.'

'They had a cloudburst over by T'isya Lani. It washed out the dam.'

'It washed out the missionary's house, they say. His wife ran out in something thin and got wet, they say.'

'*Ei-yei!*'

Tall Hunter and his wife drove past in a brand-new buckboard behind two fast-trotting, grey mules. He owned over five hundred head of horses, and his wife had thick strings of turquoise and coral around her neck.

'His brother is in jail for stealing cattle, they say.'

'What is jail?' asked Laughing Boy.

Slender Hair explained: 'It is something the American Chief does to you. He puts you in a room of stone, like a Moqui house, only it is dark and you can't get out. People die there, they say. They haven't any room; they can't see anything, they say. I do not like to talk about it.'

Laughing Boy thought, I should rather die. He wanted to ask more, but was ashamed to show his ignorance before these southern Navajos, many of whom wore hats like Americans, and who knew so much of Americans' ways.

They raced. His horse was tired, but it won by a nose, which was just as well, since he had bet his bowguard. Now he had six dollars. He hoped there would be gambling.

Tsé Lani showed a distant bonfire in the dusk, with mounted Indians moving in on it like spokes of a wheel. About two hundred young men came together half a mile away, making their ponies prance, exchanging greetings. Crooked Ear carried the ceremonial wand. Now they all lined up, with the dull, red sunset behind their black figures. They started going like getting off to a race, right into a gallop, yelling. Over by the fire was shouting, and another line tearing towards them. The world was full of a roar of hooves and two walls of noise rushing together, the men leaning forward over their horses' necks, mouths wide. *'E-e-e-e-e!'* They met in a great swirl of plunging, dodging horses, and swept on all together, whooping for dear life, with the staff in front of them, almost onto the fire, then dissolved with jingling of bits, laughter, and casual jokes as they unsaddled by the pool.

The steady motion of excitement was slowed then, in the last of the day, by the rocks and the piñons, by the reflection of the sky in the pool where flat, vague silhouettes of horses stooped to drink. The voices of many people, the twinkling of fires continued the motif, joining the time of quiet with elation past and to come; a little feeling of expectation in Laughing Boy's chest, a joyful emptiness, part hunger and part excitement.

He tended his pony minutely. The little mare had had two days of loping; shortly he wanted to race her; three days of rest would not be too much. She was his only horse; he had traded two others for her. She was tough, as a horse had to be to live at all in the North country. He ran his hands down her withers, feeling the lean, decisive muscles. In all that section, from Dennihuitso to Biltabito, from T'o Tlikahn to T'o Baka, where he knew every horse by sight, she was the best, but she would meet some competition here. He felt as if she were his own creation, like the bow-guard; at least he had selected her, as he had chosen the soft blue tur-

13

quoise in the ornament. Little, compact, all black save for the tiny white spot on her forehead, she had the ugly Roman nose of character. She was like an arrow notched to a taut bowstring—a movement of the hand would release level flight swiftly to a mark.

He was thinking some of these things, half hearing the noises of the people. Just like the prayer, 'travelling in beauty.' It would be good to be a singer as well, to express all these things through the prayers. He would like to know many of them, to learn to conduct the Mountain Chant, and know all the beautiful stories behind the songs and ceremonies inside the Dark Circle of Branches. That would be really on the trail of beauty; to work in silver and turquoise, own soft-moving ponies, and lead the Mountain Chant. Just thinking about it was good. It made him feel cool inside.

> *'Hozho hogahan ladin nasha woyen . . .*
> In the house of happiness there I wander . . .'

All the time he was passing his hand along the pony's neck, along her back, feeling the lines of tough muscles.

'*E-ya*, Grandfather, are you going to dance with the horse?' Jesting Squaw's Son called over to him, 'food is ready.'

'*Hakone!*' He returned abruptly to the quick-moving life of the dance. 'I can eat it. I did not know you were coming.'

'I came when I heard you were to race your mare. I think there is money to be made, then, and I want to see her race.'

They went up arm in arm into the crowd, pushing their way into the circle around one of the fires. Busy housewives gave them coffee, the big pot of meat was passed over, and a flat, round loaf of rubbery, filling bread. The meat was the backbone of a yearling calf, boiled with corn. It was good. He munched joyfully, feeling his empty stomach fill, wadding himself with bread, washing it down with bitter coffee. A couple of Americans carrying their own plates dipped in gingerly. A Hopi, having collected everything he could possibly eat, sat down officiously beside them to air his school English and his bourgeois superiority.

14

A small drum beating rapidly concentrated the mixed noises into a staccato unison. Young men gathered about the drummer. Laughing Boy might have eaten more, but he left the fire immediately with Jesting Squaw's Son. Some one led off high-pitched at full voice,

'Yo-o galeana, yo-o galeana, yo-o galeana . . .'

By the end of the second word the crowd was with him; more young men hurried up to join the diapason,

'Galeana ena, galeana eno, yo-o ay-e hena ena . . .'

They put their arms over each other's shoulders, swaying in time to the one drum that ran like a dull, glowing thread through the singing, four hundred young men turning loose everything they had.

A bonfire twenty feet long flared to the left of them. Opposite and to the right, the older people sat wrapped in their blankets. Behind them, men crouched in their saddles, heads and shoulders against the night sky, nodding time to the rhythm, silent, with here and there a reflection of firelight on a bit of silver, a dark face, or a horse's eye.

Twelve girls in single file stole into the open space, moving quietly and aloof as though the uproar of singing were petrified into a protective wall before it reached them. Only the pulse of the drum showed in their steps. They prowled back and forth before the line of young men, considering them with predatory judgment.

Laughing Boy at the back of the crowd looked at them with mild interest; he liked to watch their suave movements and the rich display of blankets and jewelry. One caught his attention; he thought she had on more silver, coral, turquoise, and white shell than he had ever seen on any one person. He speculated on its value—horses—she must have a very rich mother, or uncles. She was too slender, seeming frail to dance in all that rich, heavy ornamentation. He wished she would

15

move more into the firelight. She was well dressed to show off what she wore; silver and stones with soft highlights and deep shadows glowed against the night-blue velveteen of her blouse; oval plaques of silver were at her waist, and ceremonial jewels in the fringe of her sash. Her blue skirt swung with her short, calculated steps, ankle-length, above the dull red leggins and moccasins with silver buttons. The dark clothing, matching the night, was in contrast to the other dancers, even her blanket was mainly blue. He felt animosity towards her, dark and slight, like a wisp of grass—only part of a woman. Her gaze, examining the singers was too coolly appraising. Now she was looking at him. He threw his head back, losing himself in the singing. He wished he, too, had an American hat.

Her mincing steps took her out of sight. Jesting Squaw's Son's arm was over his shoulder, and on the other side another Indian, unknown, but young. Their life flowed together with all those others, complete to themselves, merged in one body of song, with the drumbeats for a heart,

'*Yo-o galeana, yo-o galeana . . .*'

Song followed song with a rush; when one ended, the next took up, as though the whole night would never suffice to pour out all that was in them.

Some one plucked at his blanket; then with another, stronger pull it was snatched from his shoulders. He whirled about. The men near him snickered. The frail girl held his blanket up toward him, mockingly.

'*Ahalani!*' she greeted him.

He stood for a moment in feigned stupidity. He did not want to dance. The devil! Then with a sudden lunge he snatched the blanket. It was no use. She hung on with unexpected strength, digging her heels into the sand, laughing. The men on either side were watching over their shoulders with open joy.

'What's the matter? I think your feet hurt, perhaps. I think you are bandy-legged, perhaps.'

Girls didn't usually say these things. He was shocked. Her clear low voice turned the insults into music, bringing out to the full the rise and fall of a Navajo woman's

16

intonation. All the time they tugged against each other, her long eyes were talking. He had seen girls' eyes talk before as they pulled at the blanket, but these were clear as words. He wanted desperately to be back among the men. He nearly pulled her over, but she hung on, and her eyes seemed to be making a fool of him.

Suddenly he gave up. She led him around behind the men, not speaking to him, uninterested. He pulled his end of the blanket over his shoulders, assuming the conventional pose of resistance, setting each foot before the other reluctantly, in response to her dragging. He watched her closely, but her grip did not slacken. Out in the clear space she transferred her hands to his belt. He pulled his blanket to his chin, masking enjoyment in a pose of contemptuous tolerance, like the other men dancing there.

The solemn turning of the couples contrasted with the free release of the singers: this was a religious cere-mony and a rustic, simple pleasure, the happiness of a natural people to whom but a few things happen. They were traditional and grave in their revelry.

According to the etiquette, whenever there is a rest, the man asks what forfeit he must pay; by the length of time taken by the girl to get down to a reasonable fig-ure, he gages her liking for his company. The music paused an instant for singers to catch their breath. He made a feeble attempt to get away, then asked,

'How much?'

'Ten cents.'

The prompt answer astonished him. He paid the forfeit, still staring at her, chagrined, and furious at the blank, correct impassiveness of her face, at the same time noting delicately chiselled features, set of firm lips, long eyes that in their lack of expression were mak-ing fun of him. Ten cents! Already! With a splendid gesture he swept his blanket round him, stalking back to the singers.

He was set to lose himself in the songs, but he watched the girl drag out a man nearly as tall as him-self. Instead of dancing in the usual way, they held each other face to face and close to, each with one hand on the other's shoulder. It was shocking; and why had she

17

not done it with him? But she had let him go the first time he had asked. She had insulted him, she was too thin, and probably ill-behaved.

III

Jesting Squaw's Son's arm was over his shoulder, his ears were full of the beat and uproar of music. He was a man among men, swinging with them, marking the rhythm, releasing his joy of living in ordered song.

'Nashdui bik'é dinni, eya-a, eyo-o . . .'

A late moon rose, cool and remote, dissociated. They brought another tree up to the bonfire, standing it on end a moment so that the hot light played on its dead branches; then they let it topple over and fall, sending up in its place a tree of moving sparks into the blackness.

Night passed its middle and stood towards day. The girls moved off together in single file, blankets drawn over heads, worn out by the night of unremitting dancing. The older people fell rapidly away. Inert forms like mummies stretched out in their blankets by the embers of the feast fires. Most of the young men gave in, leaving about a hundred knotted in a mass, still hard at it. They surrounded the drummer, an older man, intently serious over drawing forth from a bit of hide stretched across the mouth of a jar rapidly succeeding beats that entered the veins and moved in the blood. He played with rhythm as some men play with design; now a quick succession of what seemed meaningless strokes hurried forward, now the beat stumbled, paused, caught up again and whirled away. Devotedly intent over his work, his long experience, his strength and skill expended themselves in quick, wise movements of the wrist, calling forth a summation of life from a piece of goatskin and a handful of baked clay, while younger men about him swayed and rocked in recurrent crescendos.

Night stood towards morning, now night grew old. Now the first white line was traced across the east far away, outlining distant cliffs. Now it was first light, and

18

Dawn Boy was upon them. The drumming stopped; suddenly the desert was empty and vast. Young men, whose bodies felt like empty shells and whose heads still buzzed with songs, moved down to drink at the pool.

'Hayotlcatl Ashki, Natahni . . .'

Laughing Boy breathed his prayer to himself, feeling a moment of loneliness,

'Dawn Boy, Chief . . .'

He rolled up in his blanket. When he rode his horse in the races, people would see; he would ride past the people, back to T'o Tlakai, with all his winnings. That girl was strong for one who looked so slight. He would make a bracelet about her, thin silver, with stars surrounded by stone-knife-edge. His horse came to stand by him. He roused himself to look at it, struggled awake, and dragged out the corn from under his saddle.

He pulled his blanket over his head. All different things melted together into one conception of a night not like any other.

CHAPTER TWO

I

Some one was calling him,
'Eli shichai, ei-yei!'
He opened his eyes, staring upward at the face of Jesting Squaw's Son that laughed at him as he sat high above him in the saddle. The face was in shadow under

19

the circle of his stiff-brimmed hat, cut out against the gleaming, hard sky. The sun was halfway up.

'Wake up, Grandfather! Big Tall Man is going to play tree-pushing against everybody.'

'Hakone!' He was up at the word. 'Give me a smoke, Grandfather.' He climbed up behind his friend's saddle. 'Come on.'

They stopped for coffee at a hogahn near the pool, where the woman of the house mocked him for sleeping late.

The people were gathered in a little box cañon, where fire had destroyed a number of scrub oaks and piñons under one wall near a seep of water. There they were dividing into two groups, according to whether they backed Big Tall Man or Man Hammer, the policeman from over by T'o Nanasdési. Hill Singer rode back and forth between, collecting and announcing the bets. Most of the money was on Big Tall Man, and there were few takers. Laughing Boy could not place any. He saw that girl sitting among the neutral spectators.

'Who is that girl' he asked Slender Hair—'the one who had so much hard goods on last night?'

'She is called Slim Girl, I think. She comes from down by the railroad track, from near Chiziai, I think.'

Big Tall man and Man Hammer moved up to two dead trees of roughly the same size. Hill Singer and Hurries to War were judging. Now they pushed and strained at the trees, digging their feet in the sand, heaving shoulders. Big Tall Man's tree began to crack; then suddenly it went over. People exclaimed and laughed. After that nobody more wanted to play against him.

Then they had wrestling for the young men. Laughing Boy bet a little and lost a couple of dollars. There was a tall man wearing an American shirt and trousers and a hat, who made a great deal of noise about himself. He beat one challenger easily. Laughing Boy recognized the man who danced so outrageously last night.

'Who is that?' he asked.

'That is Red Man. He comes from down by the railroad.'

'He is too skinny. I am going to beat him.'

He challenged Red Man.

'How much will you bet on yourself?'

'I have three-fifty and this bow-guard.'

'That makes eight-fifty.'

'The bow-guard is worth more; it is worth ten dollars.'

The man looked at it judgingly. 'Well, it is worth eight. That makes eleven-fifty. Why don't you bet your belt?'

'It is not mine.'

'So you are sure you are going to lose, I think?'

Laughing Boy did not like this Indian. 'No; I'm going to throw you right away.'

'*Ei-yei!* Then bet the belt. See, mine is better than yours. It has turquoise in it.'

'All right.'

They piled up the stakes: three-fifty and a bow-guard against eleven-fifty, belt against belt. The belt was worth money, but it was ugly, Laughing Boy thought. He did not like this man. He knew how to dance improperly.

They stood face to face. They laid hands on each other. As he felt the man in his grasp, Laughing Boy saw all red. He and his enemy were alone in space with anger. He heaved with all his skill and strength, like one possessed. The other grunted and strained, then suddenly gave way—a fall.

Red Man arose puzzled and angry. He went at the next bout seriously. He would have liked to foul, but he was afraid of Hurries to War. Laughing Boy, staring over his opponent's shoulder, saw Slim Girl's face as she watched, half smiling. Again he ceased seeing, his jaws clamped fiercely together, he gripped close and lifted, then over—now! A fall, and a hard one.

Red Man was shaken, and came into the next bout without confidence. The fall he got was worse than the others.

'Take the goods,' Hill Singer told the winner.

'Put up your horse, and try again. You might get your belt back.' Laughing Boy mocked.

'We are going to play *Tset Dilth* on the fourth night, then bring your belts.' Red Man was feeling the back of his head.

21

"I shall be there.'

Laughing Boy gathered up his winnings. He looked around. Slim Girl had disappeared. He was hungry. He hunted up Jesting Squaw's Son.

'It is noon. Let us go eat.'

II

Many visitors were at the hogahns scattered about Tsé Lani. There was much food and much talk. Where they went, they reclined on sheepskins, while two small naked boys brought ears of corn as they were roasted, and calm women set broiled goats' ribs and corn bread before them. They ate at leisure, having a pleasant feeling of being at a party, yet at ease, and enjoying their appetites. Gossip was exchanged; they discussed crops, sheep, rain, and horses.

'I hear you have a horse to race,' a man said to Laughing Boy.

'Yes, I have a good one.'

'A man brought a tall bay over from Tsézhin; it is very fast, they say.'

'We shall see. I shall bet on my horse.'

'Where did you get your bow-guard?'

'I made it.'

'I'll give you six dollars for it.'

'I don't want to sell it.'

The man changed the subject. 'Did you hear about Red Goat? His wives put his saddle outside the door, they say.'

'What had he done?' somebody asked.

'He drank whiskey; he spent their money on it, so they say.'

'They were right, I think.'

'I have never tasted whiskey,' Laughing Boy said; 'what is it like?'

'It tastes bad, but one feels good. Then later one has a headache.'

'It sounds like t'oghlepai.'

'It is stronger. I'll give you eight dollars for that bow-guard.'

'I don't want to sell it; it is lucky.'

22

'That turquoise is no good, and the work is not very good.'

Laughing Boy looked bored. 'Give me a smoke, Grandfather.'

'The turquoise is too green. Eight dollars is a lot.'

'Eight dollars is nothing,' he answered loftily, with a pleasant remembrance of his winnings.

'Here, I have nine-fifty. That is all I have.' The man held out the money.

'No, I really do not want to sell. I would not sell it for a horse.'

'It is a fine bow-guard. If you make many things like that, you will get rich.'

Everything was well, Laughing Boy thought. He had money now, and a belt that was ugly, but could be sold to a trader for fifty dollars. People praised his work. That girl was only an incident; one should not let oneself be ruffled so easily.

It was good to lie in the sand talking a little, borrowing smokes now and then. Now that he had money, he would buy tobacco when he came to a trading post. Meantime he thought he would hunt up those two Americans to see if they would give him one of their big, white cigarettes. Perhaps they would buy his belt; they were travelling just for fun, people said; they must be rich. Perhaps, too, they would have sweet food, canned goods, and coffee with much sugar in it. He called his friend.

'Let us see if those Americans will buy my belt. Let us see what they will give us.'

'Good.'

They rode off sitting sideways on Jesting Squaw's Son's unsaddled horse, heels drumming softly on opposite sides, humming a song together.

III

The Americans, a rich Eastern tourist and his guide, were tired of feeding stray Indians, of whom there had been a plague all day. They set out to ignore these two who descended gravely upon them, but the double line of silver plaques about Laughing Boy's waist caught the tourist's eye.

'Ask him to let me see those belts,' he told the guide, and then, in baby-talk American's Navajo, 'Your belt—two—good.'

Laughing Boy sat down beside him. *'Nashto, shadani* —give me a smoke, brother-in-law.'

It is rude to call a man brother-in-law, and like most Navajos, he enjoyed using the term, and teaching it, to innocent foreigners. Americans were good fun. This one gave him a black cigar, cutting the end for him and holding out a match. It nearly killed him at the first whiff, only medicine-hogahn experience in swallowing smoke enabled him to keep a calm face.

'This is good!' He passed it over to his friend, who habitually inhaled deeply. 'It is like the magic tobacco Natinesthani gave the magician. We have nothing like this. Try it, elder brother.'

He tried it, cautiously at first, the tiniest puff, then a good lung-full that clutched his agonized insides like talons. Desperately he fought back tears and a choking cough, while Laughing Boy struggled with almost equal difficulty to keep a straight face. By a heroic effort he let the smoke out slowly. Then, with a sigh that disguised relief as critical enjoyment,

'Yes, little brother, that is very good tobacco.'

The tourist was fingering Laughing Boy's belts, pulling them around. The Indian thought of pulling in turn at his necktie, but decided it would be poor business.

'Ask him how much he wants for the one with the turquoise in it.'

'How much do you want for the one with the blues, Grandfather?' the guide asked.

'A horse, perhaps.' He puffed gingerly at the cigar which Jesting Squaw's Son passed back to him.

'I'll offer you a nickel, perhaps.'

Both laughed.

'You say, how much.'

The formal gambits were over. The guide cocked his head, pursed his lips, and looked critical and rather disgusted. 'I'll give you twenty-five dollars.'

'No, no.'

'How much, then?'

He took it off. 'This is a good belt. These stones are good. The silver is heavy; Mexican silver. That is good work. Seventy-five dollars.'

The guide grunted, and threw a pinch of sand on it in token of its worthlessness.

'What does he say he wants?'

'He says seventy-five.'

'What's it worth?'

'Up to about sixty, I guess. Them's good stones.'

'Get it for less if you can.'

Laughing Boy passed the cigar back. His friend who knew a little English whispered, 'He says sixty, I think, that he will pay.' He blew out on the cigar to use up as much as was possible.

Laughing Boy asked the guide, 'Where do you come from?'

'From Besh Senil. We are going to the Moqui.'

'*Ei-yei!* That's far! Why do you want to see the Moqui?'

'We want to see them dance with snakes.'

'They are crazy to do that. Our dances are better.'

'Perhaps. Well, this man says your belt is pretty good, and he will give you forty for it. No more.'

'No, seventy, no less.' He buckled it on again.

'Perhaps we can give you forty-five, but that is all.'

Laughing Boy took the cigar again. It was a long time burning down. He wondered if he would die and be brought to life again, like the magician who smoked with Natinesthani.

'What does the Indian want?' the tourist asked.

'He still says seventy; it's too much.'

'Get it if you can.'

Laughing Boy whispered, 'What are they saying, Grandfather?'

'I'm not sure. That one who speaks Navajo says "too much," I think. The pink one says "get it." '

The guide spoke to them. 'This man says he will give you fifty because he likes your belt. He cannot give any more.'

'No, I do not want to sell. He does not want to pay what it is worth, he is just talking about wanting it.' The cigar was done at last. He rose.

'Oh, give him what he wants!'

"How much, Grandfather? You say.'

'Sixty-five, perhaps.'

'He says sixty-five. Looks like he won't come down no lower.'

'I'll take it.'

'He says he'll take it.'

Laughing Boy handed over the belt. 'Grandfather, do you know this paper money?'

Jesting Squaw's Son considered the bills. 'Yes, these with tracks here in the corners are fives. These with little sticks and the man with long hair and the ugly mouth on them are ones. This with the yellow back, I do not know it. I think it is no good.' He had been stung once on cigar coupons.

At last the sum was made up, with ones, fives, and the silver dollars which they preferred.

'Ask that man,' Laughing Boy told the guide, 'to give us another of those big, black cigarettes. They are good.'

The guide translated.

'My God! I thought it would make them sick. Here's one for each of them.'

'Good. Now, Grandfather, give me some cigarette papers.'

The guide forked up. As they shook hands all around, elaborately, Navajo fashion, the Americans' faces and voices seemed to grow very distant and uncertain. Riding away, Laughing Boy sighed deeply.

'Let us go to a quiet place. I want to be sick.'

'I too.'

Later, at sunset, they went to wash at the pool, dipping up liquid silver and lilac in their hands. They lay back against the rock watching the sun go down, the shadows and lights on the water, the distant fires and people moving. They had slept, they felt very empty, clean, and peaceful.

'Shall we try making a cigarette with that tobacco?'

'Not yet, I think. Go tend your horse. It is time to eat again.'

'I go. I hope there will be much gambling after this.'

CHAPTER THREE

I

THE dance of the second night was much like that of the first, although perhaps a little less exuberant. He entered once more into the river of song, and was happy, yelling his head off, save that he kept on being conscious of that girl. While she was dancing, he would forget about her, but when he saw her looking for another partner, he would be uneasy until she had made her choice. He noticed that she did not dance with Red Man. Halfway between midnight and dawn, the women having departed, he fell out, to sleep by a fire.

They rode down to Ane'é Tseyi that day, where the dance of the final night would be held. He rode behind Jesting Squaw's Son's saddle, leading the mare. He hoped they would find a place with some grass for the animal, and reflected that in any case, now, he could afford to buy corn. The long, hot ride, hot sun, hot wind, unrelieved, weighed on them somewhat, combining with lack of sleep to make limbs sluggish and eyes heavy. It was a relief to ride into the narrow cañon of their destination, to rest in a strip of afternoon shade. Laughing Boy took the horses down to the windmill for water, and staked them out in a corner where uncropped spears of grass stood singly, each inches from the next, in brown sand. A beaten track toward an oak tree and a break in the rock caught his eye. A spring, perhaps.

He followed it. Behind the oak, currant bushes grew in a niche of red rock like the fold of a giant curtain. At the back was a full-grown, lofty fir. A spring, surely. Behind the fir a cleft opened at shoulder height into transparent shadow. The footholds were worn to velvety roundness in the sandstone; at one side a pecked design showed that long before the Navajos had swooped upon the land, a people of an elder earth had known this entrance. Laughing Boy climbed lightly in.

It was a stone-lined pocket, scarce twenty feet across, narrower at the top. One went forward along a ledge at one side, shouldering against young aspens, then slid down a rock face into a curving bowl, with a seep at one lip from which silent water oozed over moss and cress into the bottom. Spears of grass grew in cracks. By the tiny pool of water in the bowl was a square of soft turf with imprints of moccasins. He squatted there, leaning back against the rock. Here was all shade and peace, soft, grey stone, dark, shadowed green, coolness, and the sweet smell of dampness. He dabbled his hands, wet his face, drank a little. He rolled a cigarette with crumpled cigar tobacco. This was good, this was beautiful.

Away above, the intolerant sky gleamed, and a corner of cloud was white fire. His eyes shifting lightly, the edge of the rocks above took on a glowing halo. He amused himself trying to fit it back again, to get the spot the cloud made back against the cloud, playing tricks with his half-closed eyelashes that made things seem vague.

'*Ahalani!*' The two-toned greeting came from a voice like water.

He returned to himself with a start. Slim Girl stood poised on the edge of the bowl, above his shoulder, water-basket in hand.

'*Ahalani, shicho.*' Dignified, casual.

'Move over, wrestler, I want to come down.'

He observed her small feet in their red, silver-buttoned buckskin, sure and light on the rocks as a goat's. She seemed to be hours descending. She was businesslike about filling the basket, but she turned utilitarian motions into part of a dance. Now she knelt, not two feet from him, taking him in with the long, mischievous eyes that talked and laughed.

She is a butterfly, he thought, or a hummingbird. Why does she not go away? I will not go—run away from her. He thought, as he tried to read her face, that her slimness was deceptive; strength came forth from her.

'Now, for ten cents, I go.'

He blinked. 'I save that to get rid of you tonight, perhaps.'

'I do not dance to-night. There is trouble, a bad thing. I come from far away.'

He thought he had better not ask questions. 'To-morrow there will be horse-racing, a chicken-pull, perhaps.'

'And you have a fine horse to race, black, with a white star and a white sock.' He grunted astonishment. She smiled. 'You are a good jeweler, they say. You made that bow-guard. You sold Red Man's belt to the American, they say, for sixty-five dollars.'

'You are like an old wife, trying to find out about everything a man is doing.'

'No, I am not like an old wife.'

They looked at each other for a long time. No, she was not like an old wife. Blood pounded in his ears and his mouth was dry. He pulled at the end of his dead cigarette. At length,

'You should stay for the racing. There will be fine horses, a beautiful sight.'

'I shall stay, perhaps.'

Her rising, her ascent of the rock, were all one quick motion. She never looked back. He stayed, not exactly in thought, but experiencing a condition of mind and feeling. Loud laughter of women roused him, to pass them with averted eyes and go forth dazed into the sunlight.

II

The last night of the dance was a failure for Laughing Boy, for all its ritual. He tried to join the singing, but they were not the kind of songs he wanted; he tried to concentrate on the prayer that was being brought to a climax, but he wanted to pray by himself. He quit the dance, suddenly very much alone as he left the noise and the light behind him, strongly conscious of himself, complete to himself. He followed a sheep trail up a break in one cañon wall, to the rim, then crossed the narrow mesa to where he could look down over the broad Ties Hatsosi Valley, a great pool of night, and far-distant, terraced horizon of mesas against the bright stars, cool, alone, with the sound of the drumming and music behind him, faint as memory. This also was a form of living.

He began to make up a new song, but lost interest in it, feeling too centred upon himself. He sat noticing little things, whisper of grass, turn of a leaf—little enough there is in the desert at night.

> *'Yota zhil-de tlin-sha-igahl . . .'*

His song came upon him.

> *'A-a-a-ainé, ainé.*
> I ride my horse down from the high hills
>   To the valley, *a-a-a.*
> Now the hills are flat. Now my horse will not go
>   From your valley, *a-a-a.*
> *Hainéya, ainé, o-o-o-o.'*

Slim Girl sat down beside him. His song trailed off, embarrassed. They rested thus, without words, looking away into the night while contemplation flowed between them like a current. At length she raised one hand, so that the bracelets clinked.

'Sing that song.'

He sang without effort. This was no common woman, who ignored all convention. The long-drawn *'Hainéya, ainé, o-o-o-o-'* fell away into the lake of darkness; silence shut in on them again.

On the heels of his song he said, 'My eldest uncle is here. I am going to speak to him tomorrow.'

'I should not do that if I were you.'

He rolled a cigarette with careful movements, but forbore to light it. Again they sat watching the motionless stars above the shrouded earth. No least breeze stirred; there were no details to be seen in the cliffs or the valley, only the distant silhouettes against the sky. A second time her hand rose and her bracelets clinked, as though speech unannounced would startle the universe.

'You are sure you are going to speak to your uncle, then?'

'Yes.' The second self that is a detached mentor in one's mind recognized that he would never have talked this way with any other woman. Etiquette had been left behind down in the narrowness of Ane'é Tseyi.

'Perhaps you will listen to what he says, I think; perhaps you will not. Perhaps your mind is made up now.'

'I am thinking about what I intend to do. I shall not change.'

'We shall see then. Good-bye.'

She rose like smoke. He called a startled 'Good-bye,' then began to follow at a distance. He stopped at the rim of the cañon, where the noise of singing that welled up from below passed him by as he stood watching her dark form, down to the bottom, along by the grove where his camp was, and beyond into the shadows.

He went back to the far edge of the mesa. He did not want to sleep, not ever again.

'Now with a god I walk,
Now I step across the summits of the mountains,
Now with a god I walk,
Striding across the foothills.
Now on the old age trail, now on the path of beauty
       wandering.
In beauty—*Hozoji, hozoji, hozoji-i.*'

The deep resonance of the prayer carried his exaltation through the land. Then he began to analyse her words, finding in them nothing save unconventionality, no promise, and his own he found laggard and dull. Was she playing with him, or did she mean all he read into her brevity? Was she thus with other men?

'I ride my horse down from the high hills
    To the valley, *a-a-a . . .*'

He was up and down, restless, no longer on the path of beauty, yet tormented by a new beauty. Far away, high-pitched, he heard the faint '*Yo-o galeana, yo-o galeana,*' and the thudding drum. He walked to and fro. My mind is made up, I shall make things as they should be. Now with a god I walk—or is it a game, looseness?

Suddenly he fled to sleep for refuge, rolling in his

blanket by a high place under thickly clustered, brilliant, unhelpful stars, falling asleep with the feeling of vastness about him and clean, gracious silence.

III

He woke to a feeling of expectation, and made his dawn Prayer with all the gladness that his religion prescribed. He could not wait to see his uncle and have the matter settled before they went to the trading post for the races. At the same time, his own certainty told him that his eldest uncle, his mother, and all her kin were only wanted to ratify a decision already made. What was, was; he would announce what he wanted to do, not ask for permission.

Now he stood on the rim above the cañon, bathed in sunlight, while below him in thick, visible shadow unimportant people moved, horses stamped, smoke rose from tiny fires.

His uncle was staying down by the trading post with Killed a Navajo. He started off without breakfast, leading the pony, and sorely tempted to mount and gallop those few miles, but the thought of the race and the pleasure of winning restrained him. I'll win for Slim Girl, he thought with a smile, and burst into song, lustily pouring forth keen delight from tough lungs over the empty flat. The dusty walk and hot sun, the heat that lay over the baked adobe and dull sagebrush, troubled him not at all. The bleak, grey parts of the desert have a quintessential quality of privacy, and yet one has space there to air one's mood. So Laughing Boy sang loudly, his horse nosed his back, a distant turtle-dove mocked him, and a high-sailing, pendent buzzard gave him up as far too much alive.

Killed a Navajo's hogahn was well built, of thick-laid evergreens over stout piñon poles. Looking in through the wide door one was conscious of cool darkness flecked with tiny spots of light, a central brilliance under the smoke-hole, vague outlines of reclining figures, their feet, stretched towards the centre, grotesquely clear. He stood in the doorway. Some one spoke to him, 'Come in.' He shook hands all round. They offered him a little coffee, left over from breakfast, and tobacco. He made himself comfortable on the sheepskins beside his uncle in the place of honour.

One by one the family went about their work; the children to tend the sheep, Killed a Navajo down to the store where he did odd jobs, and was needed to-day for distributing free food, his younger wife to preparing a meal for the many guests expected that day, his first wife to weaving, outside. Laughing Boy's cigarette smoke went up in shadow, was caught in a pencil of sunlight, disappeared, and gleamed once again before it seeped through the roof. A suggestion of a breeze rustled the green walls. He studied his uncle's face—big and massive, with heavy high-bridged nose and deep furrows enclosing the wide, sure mouth. Under the blue turban wisps of hair showed a little grey. Across his cheek-bone ran the old scar from which he took his name, Wounded Face. It was an old eagle's head. Laughing Boy was a little afraid of it.

'My uncle.'

'Yes, my child.' The old-fashioned, round silver ear-rings shimmered faintly.

'I have been thinking about something.'

They smoked on. A black-and-white kid slipped in the door, leaped up and poised itself on the cantle of a saddle. Outside was the rhythmic thump-thump-thump of a weaver pounding down the threads in her loom. A distant child laughed, some one was chopping wood—sounds of domesticity.

'I have been thinking about a wife.'

'You are old enough. It is a good thing.'

He finished his cigarette.

'You know that Slim Girl? The one who wears so much hard goods? She danced the first two nights.'

'She is a school-girl.' The tone was final. 'She was taken away to that place, for six years.'

'That is all right. I like her.'

'That is not all right. I do not know how she came to be allowed to dance. They made her stop. Water Singer let her dance, but we stopped him. She is bad. She lives down by the railroad. She is not of the People any more, she is American. She does bad things for the Americans.'

'I do not know what you mean, but I know her, that

33

girl. She is not bad. She is good. She is strong. She is for me.'

'You come from away up there; you do not know about these things. Nor do you know her. What is her clan?'

'I do not know.'

'Well? And what makes you think you can go out and pick a wife for yourself like this? The next thing I know, you will jump into the fire. I tell you, she is all bad; for two bits she will do the worst thing.'

Laughing Boy sat up suddenly. 'You should not have said that, you should not have thought it. Now you have said too much. I hope that bad thing follows you around always. Now you have said too much. Ugh! This place is too small for me!'

He ran outside. He needed space. People were beginning to arrive; there was laughing and shouting around the trading post. He went off rapidly to get by himself, too proud to run before people. His mind was boiling; he wanted to hit something, he was all confused. This way he went on until at last he reached a small butte that offered protection. He tore around the corner.

Slim Girl was walking towards him, cool and collected. Her brows rose in surprise as she stopped. He came up to her uncertainly.

'Sit down; there is shade here.' They faced each other. 'You have seen your uncle.'

His hand fell forward in the gesture of assent.

'And he spoke to you.'

'He said bad things. I am angry with him.'

'And towards me?'

'You came here on purpose to meet me.'

'Yes; I knew that when you had seen your uncle, you should see me soon.'

'What my uncle said will stay with him. He has made a bad thing, it will follow him. The track of an evil thought is crooked and has no end; I do not want it around me; I do not keep it going. I have only good thoughts about you.'

'Your mother will never send some one to ask for me. You must just come with me.'

'Wait; what is your clan?'

'I am a Bitahni; and you?'

34

'Tahtchini; so that is all right. But I have nothing to give your mother, only one horse.'

'I have no parents; they died when I was at school. I belong to myself. All this'—she raised the necklaces, turquoise, coral, white shell and silver, one by one, then let them fall back together—'is mine. All this'—she touched her rings, and shook her braceletted wrists— 'and much more is mine. They left it for me. Now I do a little work for the missionary's wife there at Chiziai; she pays me money, so I grow richer. I shall give you silver to make jewelry, and I shall weave, and you shall have fine horses. You can make money with them, and we shall be rich together.'

The long, talking eyes looked into his now, with nothing hidden. He felt her strength, this woman who could talk so straight, who made the direct road seem the only sensible one. It ceased to be strange that they sat and talked about love, while elopement became obvious and commonplace in a scheme of things the whole of which was suddenly miraculous.

After a while she said, 'We shall go tonight, after the races.'

He reflected. 'No, I came here to gamble. I told Red Man I would play against him. If I do not do it, he will say I am afraid.'

'He is crooked; he will take your money.'

'That makes no difference; I cannot back down now. If I let this go because I was afraid to lose, what would I be? If I refused because of you, what kind of a man should I be for you?'

He saw that he had spoken well.

'It will be time for the races soon; you must go. I go the other way round.'

He was in a new and more profound daze returning, but yards that had seemed miles were passed as inches. He floated over the ground, he was a walking song.

CHAPTER FOUR

I

THE horses-races were to be held in the latter part of the afternoon; during the hottest time almost everybody took a siesta, while those who were entering horses tended to them. Jesting Squaw's Son joined Laughing Boy in going over the black pony. They discussed the other entries, agreeing that competition would be severe. A man from Navajo Mountain, in old-fashioned fringed buckskin skirt and high leggins, had brought a dun mare, said to be swift as thought. Jesting Squaw's Son had seen her; she moved beautifully, he said. From Tsézhin came the undefeated bay, and the local contender, a big iron-grey, had a good reputation. Its sire was an American stallion, it was long in the quarters, and relatively heavy-boned; Laughing Boy thought that in a short race-course—the usual Navajo track is under a quarter of a mile—it could not do justice to itself.

Laughing Boy planned to bet a little on the saddle-changing race, and put the rest of his money on himself. His friend would bet here and there, though mostly on him.

'Are you going into the chicken-pull?' Jesting Squaw's Son asked.

'Why not? That one race won't tire my pet.'

'But the chicken-pull will come first, they say.'

'That's bad. Why is that?'

'That man from Tsézhin, his horse got loose, they say. He is out tracking it. So your race will be held last, to let him be in it.'

'The devil! Then I can't go in the chicken-pull.

I won't risk having something happen to spoil this one. And you?'

'I shall go in.'

All the time they talked so, Laughing Boy was thinking, how do I do this? I am talking about the same things, thinking about them. And I am the man who is going away with that girl tomorrow. I am going away with Slim Girl. I feel like shouting. I am not as all these people.

Jesting Squaw's Son noticed something in his manner. 'You seem very eager, my friend.'

'Why not? Is not all well? I trade everything I have, two ponies, a blanket, five dollars, for this one because I love a fine pony, because I think this one is better than all that. Then I come down here, and right away I make nearly ninety dollars, when I began with nothing. Now we have a race. Nothing is more beautiful than galloping as hard as you can. I do this thing, that I love, on this pony that I bought for pleasure, where many people'— and one person, oh, beautiful!—'may see and speak well of me. If I win, I double my money, for doing what I enjoy. If I lose, it is only what I never had until yesterday.'

And whatever happens, I have won more than all the money and hard goods in the world.

He meant what he said. Jesting Squaw's Son nodded.

There was a shot. The pony jumped. Then two shots together, from somewhere over to the right. Hastily tethering the animal, they raced to their camp to get their bows. People were running all about; women gathering around the camp-fires, packing up bundles, men snatching their weapons and making towards the noise. Three more shots had been fired, about ten seconds apart. The men did not rush towards the firing as Americans would; they went rapidly, but keeping a sharp look-out, and ready to take cover. Some one shouted that a Hopi had killed a Navajo; some one else called that it was Americans. Now they heard a burst of quick shooting, both rifles and revolvers, at a greater distance. Topping a slight ridge, the two friends saw the Navajos just ahead, nearly a hundred already, in an irregular, slightly crescent-shaped line. They came up and pushed to the front. No one was talking.

About twenty paces in front, facing the crescent, stood Tall Old One, the district headman, and an American from the agency in army hat, riding-breeches, and leather leggins. The American had a rifle and a revolver. Behind these two, in open order, stood Man Hammer and Left Hand, policemen, and a Hopi and a Tewa policeman, all with rifles. The latter two wore parts of khaki uniforms. Over to one side a Navajo leant against a tree, looking sick. Blood ran down his sleeve and dripped from his fingers; at his feet lay a revolver. Farther back another policeman, Mud's Son, stood guard over a handcuffed Navajo, and, partly hidden by a clump of bushes, somebody was stretched out on the ground.

The American official and the Hopi were acutely conscious of the fact that several hundred Navajos were thinking that these aliens had started something, and if only the native officials would step aside it might as well be finished now. They also knew that those same officials were aware of this feeling, and sympathized with it. There were a couple of dozen rifles and revolvers in the crowd, and at that range a bow is just as effective. The Indians were all looking at the wounded man; he made an ugly exhibit.

The Tewa policeman shifted from foot to foot and grinned. The situation might become serious, but he thought it would work out all right, and he devoutly hoped for an arrest involving a fist-fight with a Navajo. Tewas punch; Navajos kick, scratch, and pull hair. For several centuries the Tewas' official profession was fighting Navajos.

Nobody knew quite what had happened. A Navajo was arrested, and one was wounded. There was a dead man, but they couldn't see of what tribe. The older men hoped there would be no trouble; nothing to bring soldiers into the reservation; the younger braves all wanted to start something. Men began to sidle off to the left and right, slowly carrying the horns of the crescent farther around the police. In time, they would have them surrounded.

Tall Old One called: 'Wait! Make no mistake! Everything is well and you have no cause to be angry.'

They obeyed him, and the tension relaxed slightly.

A man said, 'There come some more people.'
Another cried, 'An American is hurt!'
People felt better immediately.
'Two Americans—look!'

They began to talk excitedly, and some of them smiled. The government man let out a sigh and threw this gun across his left arm. Man Hammer said something cheerful to Left Hand.

The newcomers arrived from the direction of the burst of shots that had been fired last. Thin American, the trader from Tséchil, and an unknown Navajo supported between them a badly wounded man who swore slowly and steadily. Behind them a Tewa supported another American official, who limped.

They set the wounded men down by the handcuffed Navajo, the Tewa lined up beside his fellow tribesman, and Thin American came to talk with the official. After a minute of discussion, he interpreted to Tall Old One.

The headman stepped forward.

'Hear me, my friends. You know how bad it is to drink whiskey, how it makes you crazy. You know how Washindon has forbidden it. Now the American here, this man whom you have seen brought in, came here to sell it. That Navajo'—he pointed to the handcuffed one—'came with him. That was bad. So American Chief sent these Americans and policemen to stop it.'

As he talked, Thin American translated to the agency man.

'Already one man was drunk; that wounded one over there by the tree. See what it did for him. When we started to arrest them, he began to shoot. He killed that Hopi you see back there.'

So it was a Hopi killed. There were more smiles.

'Now he and this man, the one who helped to sell it, and that man must all go to jail. You know it is right. There is nothing to upset you; there is nothing to spoil your races. After all, there has been a Hopi killed, and two Americans wounded; now an American and two Navajos go to jail for a little while. That is not so bad.'

The trader suppressed a smile as he skipped translating this last remark, saying only, 'He's letting 'em think that Indian will only get a light sentence for shooting the policeman. Best leave it at that.'

Older men remarked, 'That is right, that is well said. Let us have no trouble.' Some of the young men grumbled, but others asked them, 'What would you do? You can't fight Washindon. Do you want them to send soldiers in here again? Shall we go into exile again?' It was news, an incident, something to talk about. The crowd became just a lot of people, watching the first aid, and talkative.

'Have the Hopi and Tewas take off that dead man,' the trader advised; 'they'll never forgive you if you leave a corpse for them to take care of; spoil their party and make 'em leave. They're plumb scared to death of a corpse. Look how those Navajo policemen are edging away from it.'

Horses were brought up, the wounded and prisoners mounted. The Pueblo policemen slung their comrade's body across a saddle. The party rode off, leaving Tall Old One and the local police to return to their games.

The first Tewa remarked to the other, 'No fight.'

'No. But it would have been more shooting anyhow.'

'Some day, perhaps, we arrest an American, unwounded.'

'Some day, perhaps.'

They looked at their knuckles.

II

The two friends returned to the pony.

'What is this whiskey?' Jesting Squaw's Son asked. 'I am always hearing talk about it. They say it is so bad, yet they try so hard to get it.'

'I do not know. They all say it is very bad. It makes you crazy, they say. It must be like eating jimpsonweed I think.'

'It made that man crazy. He tried to fight alone.'

'M-m. It made him brave, I think. But it stopped his sense. When a thing like that happens, a number of men coming against you, you run away first. Then you can get behind something and start shooting.'

'Anyhow, he killed a Hopi.'

'*Ei-yei!* He shot straight! But jail is very bad, they say.'

'Well, that's just for a few months, and he will have that to think about. When he comes back, people will think well of him.'

The call sounded for the first race, which was the saddle-changing relay. They separated in the crowd, which split into two parties according to whom it backed. Laughing Boy put two dollars on a group of active young men with a short-coupled pony that looked as if it could turn smartly and not get flustered.

The ponies were saddled and mounted. The cinch-strap was carried through the ring of the girth, then up the horn, where the rider held it fast with one hand, a finger of which also hooked in the reins. The other hand held a quirt ready to strike. The men were stripped to breech-clout and moccasins, slender, golden-brown bodies, the bodies of perfect boys, under the dark colour a glow of red showing through.

Now! The ponies scampered, people shouted. The horsemen flashed to earth, bringing their saddles with them, the ponies were wheeled around. Bare arms and backs rippled as the new saddles were swung on, the cinch-strap caught through, held to the horn by the same hand on which the new rider swung as he leaped to the saddle, the horse already in motion under him.

A man's foot slipped. Every one laughed and cheered. It was a close race. Now the last men were mounting. The one on the team Laughing Boy was backing lost his grip on the strap, and the saddle turned under him. He wrenched it back, throwing his weight in the stirrups, then clinched his legs under the horse's belly. But he had thrown his mount out of its stride, and he lost by a good length. They laughed more, and called jokes to him,

'Grease on your fingers, Grandfather! You should have held the strap in your teeth!'

Laughing Boy went to pay his bet. They were organizing the chicken-pull. The chicken was a salt-bag half full of dirt. A piece of blue cloth tied around its neck was the head; two bits of red at the bottom corners were the legs. Whoever threw the head over the line, a hundred yards away, won five dollars; each of the legs brought two.

Laughing Boy drifted around the edge of the crowd,

41

gay and excited. Never had there been such a four days! He had an eye out for Slim Girl, and saw her at last, sitting slightly apart from a group of women. Their eyes met, then he moved away.

Red Man hailed him. 'You are racing a horse. Grandfather?'

'Yes.'

'I hope you win. I shall take it all away from you tonight.'

'All right.'

He turned out of the crowd to avoid him; the man made him feel disagreeable. Towards him walked a pinto pony with too-long ears, carrying Half Man, his father's brother. Laughing Boy watched him sorrowfully as he approached, considering the withered arm and leg, the wasted appearance of this man, and remembering Wolf Killer, the tall, cheerful brave he had known as a boy, before the Ute arrow grazed the right side of his head and, by some strange Ute magic, shrivelled the left side of his body.

'*Ahalani*, nephew. Are you here alone?'

'Yes. It is good to see you.'

'Are all well?'

'All are well, but there has been very little rain this spring.'

'Too bad. The chicken-pull is starting. Aren't you in it?'

'I have only one horse; that I am riding in the last race.'

'You should be in it. I should have been in it at your age. This horse is all right; take it.'

He dismounted clumsily, taking a walking-stick from behind the saddle. Laughing Boy felt his eyes sting.

'*Ukehé*, Thank you.'

Navajos almost never say thank you, save in return for very great favours; ordinary gifts and kindnesses are offered and accepted in silence. They regard our custom as obsequious. The word was startled out of Laughing Boy by the occasion. Half Man understood, and avoided his nephew's gaze as he limped away, the fingers of his useless arm hooked into the front of his silver belt.

The chicken was buried in loose earth, so that just

42

enough of the neck of the sack stuck up to let one get a good grip. A referee stood near, armed with a long horsehair quirt; as each horseman rode past, he swung full force across the animal's rump, thus ensuring an honest gallop. Laughing Boy cantered up in his turn, tried to hold his pony in, felt it leap to the smack of the whip, and reached too late for the prize. He watched the next few tries, rode back, argued with Slender Hair about his place, and went at it again. He was leaning well down from the saddle before the quirt fell, he could have touched the ground with his fingers. Smack! and the pony jumped slightly sideways. The chicken was out of reach. He swung back to his seat and rested. Horse after horse came by, well in hand, then leaped to the stroke of the whip, or shied away from it. The horsemen swooped, swinging incredibly low, reaching amazingly far out, in a haze of dust.

Ya-hai! E-ya-hai! Ei-yei! Straight Fingers had it. Straight Fingers galloped for the line. All the young men rose in their saddles, their elbows were spread forward, their knees clutched, their quirts fell on willing ponies. Those who had been waiting just for this headed him off, the others caught up with him. It became a big, spinning wheel of mounted braves, horses' tossing heads, and dust. Laughing Boy saw Straight Fingers just ahead of him, clinging to the chicken's head, while some one else held both its legs. He took a lick at the next horse in front of him, saw it carom, and reached for the prize, yelling. Somebody cracked him over the head with the butt of a quirt; somebody else tried to pull him off. He defended himself, wrestling with the man who had grabbed him, while the two ponies plunged, then both let go as the mob swirled away from them.

Straight Fingers broke away, and threw the head over the line. Somebody else threw over both legs. Laughing Boy and the stranger, a young fellow with a mustache, laughed at each other.

'This has been a lovely day!' said the young man.

'Yes, a perfect day!'

'Aren't you the man from T'o Tlakai who has a horse to race? Is *that* the horse?'

43

'I'm the man. This is not the horse.'

And I am the man whom that girl loves, I am the man who is going away with the magic girl.

III

The man from Tsézhin had found his horse; now the last race was called. Laughing Boy placed everything except his bow-guard in bets. If he won, he would have nearly two hundred dollars. Now he stripped off his clothes to his breechclout, settled his headband, and adjusted the light hackamore around his horse's nose.

They gathered at the starting place, good horses and eager, with shiny coats, erect ears, and quick, small hooves. Hurries to War, the starting judge, cautioned them. Laughing Boy saw Slim Girl, halfway down the track, watching him.

Here I am doing just this, and these others do not know who I am. They do not know they are racing against the man who goes with her tomorrow. Oh, I must win, I want to win, I must win!

He made a very brief prayer, and patted his pony's neck. 'Little sister, we must win. Do not fail me.'

They mounted. He felt the warm, silky hide between his knees, pushed her up to the reins and felt the play of muscles. Counting for the start; he leant forward, held his breath, raised his quirt. Go!

Arrows from the bow—no other simile. At the tearing gallop, flat-stretched, backs are level, the animals race in a straight line; all life is motion; there is no body, only an ecstasy; one current between man and horse, and still embodied, a whip hand to pour in leather and a mouth to shout. Speed, speed, but the near goal is miles away, and other speed spirits on either side will not fall back.

E-é-é-é-é! His left hand, held forward, would push the horse through slack reins, his heels under her belly would lift her clear of the ground. *E-é-é-é-é!*

A quiet, elderly Indian let his hand fall. The ponies cantered, trotted, were turned and walked back to the finish.

'The black mare was first.'

He rode off to his camp, to dress. We won. I am rich. Was there ever such a day? And to-morrow I go with that girl. Oh, beautiful! I wish it were to-morrow now. About a hundred and eighty dollars. My pet, my little black pet, well done. I wish it were to-morrow.

CHAPTER FIVE

I

LAUGHING BOY went off alone to wrestle with gods: Slim Girl turned to loneliness as a tried friend and counsellor. To be with herself, complete to herself, that was familiar reality; distraction and strangeness was to be among many, to consult. On a high place she sat down to think, not facing the greatness of the desert, but where she could look on her gathered people, made small and impersonal below her. Long habit and self-training had made her cool and contained; she did not like to admit that she had need of mere emotion, and when she did allow herself a luxury of feeling, it had to be where none could spy on her. It was not that she would make any demonstration; she just did not want to be looked at when she was not quite mistress of herself. Now her isolated, high position put a physical difference between her impulses and those of the people in the valley, making them visibly superior. She lit a cigarette and relaxed.

If she did not watch out, she would love this man. She did not intend to love any one; had she not learned enough of that? He was necessary to her; he was the perfect implement delivered to her hands; he was an axe with which to hew down the past; he was a light with which to see her way back to her people, to the

45

good things of her people. She held him up against the past, matrons and teachers at school, platitudes and well-meaning lies. And now, for all their care and training and preaching, she was 'going back to the blanket,' because under the blanket were the things worth while, and all the rest was hideous. With her knowledge and experience, with what the Americans had taught her, she would lead this man, and make for them both the most perfect life that could be made—with an Indian, a long-haired, heathen Indian, a blanket Indian, a Navajo, the names thrown out like an insult in the faces of those who bore them, of her own people, Denné, The People, proud as she was proud, and clear of heart as she could never be.

There were to be no mistakes, and no chances. She could tie this man to her as surely as any prisoner; she would follow her clear plan to its victorious end. She had conquered herself, she had conquered circumstance; emerging from the struggle not American, not Indian, mistress of herself. Now from the Americans she took means, and in the Indians would achieve her end. Not such an amazing end, perhaps, but strange enough for her: a home in the Northern desert, and children, in a place where the agent's men never came to snatch little children from their parents and send them off to school. They would be Navajo, all Navajo, those children, when the time came. This was her revenge, that all the efforts of all those very different Americans to drag her up or to drag her down into the American way, in the end would be only tools to serve a Navajo end.

It made her happy to think of that man, Laughing Boy. He was more than just what that name implied; one felt the warrior under the gaiety, and by his songs and his silver, he was an artist. All Navajo, even to his faults, he would teach her the meaning of those oft-repeated phrases, *'bik'é hojoni,* the trail of beauty'; through him she would learn the content, and she would provide the means.

Yes, this was her man, as though he had been made expressly for her, strong, straight, gay, a little stubborn. He had character, she would develop it. And she would bind him. There would be no second wife in her hogahn.

46

'Patience,' she told herself; 'you are not in the Northern desert yet. You have a long road to travel yet, full of ambushes.'

She had no intention of herding sheep and slaving away her youth in a few years of hard labour, herding sheep, hoeing corn, packing firewood, growing square across the hips and flat in the face and heavy in the legs. No; she had seen the American women. First there was money; the Americans must serve her a little while yet; then, after that, the unmapped cañons, and the Indians who spoke no English.

She sat perfectly still, looking at nothing and hating Americans. She had not turned herself loose like this in a long time. Some young man, far below, was singing a gay song about the owl that turned her thoughts to Laughing Boy; she relaxed and smiled. This was something happy to think of. He came like the War God in the song, she thought, and began to sing it haltingly, not sure of the exact words—

'Now Slayer of Enemy Gods, alone I see him coming;
Down from the skies, alone I see him coming.
His voice sounds all about. *Lé-é!*
His voice sounds, divine. *Lé-é!*'

That is he, she thought, Slayer of Enemy Gods. He would be shocked to hear me say it, to hear a woman sing that song.

She went on to the formal ending, 'In beauty it is finished, in beauty it is finshed,' then changed it, 'In beauty it is begun. In beauty it is begun. Thanks.'

That is a good religion, as good as Christianity. I wonder if I can learn to believe in it? One needs some religion. At least, I can get good out of its ideas. If he is that god, what am I? White Shell Woman? Changing Woman, perhaps. I must mould and guide this War God I have made. I must not let him get away from me. None of the bad things must happen; I must make no mistakes. I am not a Navajo, nor am I an American, but the Navajos are my people.

II

The sun was low; the shadow sides of cliffs became deep pools of violet seeping out across the sand. She

47

rose and drew her blanket about her, composing herself for contacts with intrusive humanity. Down the steep trail her little, moccasined feet sought the sure footholds lightly. Above her feet, the clumsy deerskin leggins were thick; the heavy blanket gave a quaint stiffness to her body. Wrapped so, her feet and head and slender hands alone showing, she became pathetically small, a wisp; but her thoughtful eyes were not pathetic.

The American guide hailed her as she passed his camp, using her school name, 'Hi, there, Lily!' She dismissed him with a measuring glance that made his backbone feel cool.

'God-damnedest la-dee-dah squaw I ever run acrost!'

She had little appetite, but camped with a group of distant relatives all too ready to look askance at her, she took pains to do the normal, which was to sup well. She helped with the cooking, dipped into the pot of mutton, drank coffee, then rolled a cigarette. The Indians joked and laughed without reducing the speed of their eating. Chunks of meat and bits of squash were scooped, dripping, from the pot, to be compounded with bread into appalling, mouth-filling tidbits. Three coffee cups and a Hopi bowl served for all to drink in turn; a large spoon was purely a cooking implement. They sprawled on a half-circle of sheepskins within the open brush shelter, facing the fire, chattering and joking. Still in holiday mood, they heaped the blaze high, lighting up the circle and throwing lights that were ruddy, soft shadows on the bushes roundabout.

Some of them prepared to sleep. Visitors dropped in; more coffee was made. Slim Girl drew apart, into the darkness, and rolled up. Over there, a chink of light showed in the blanketed door of a big, earth-covered winter hogahn. Singing came out of it, rollicking, running songs. They were gambling there; Laughing Boy would soon be penniless. She smiled at the thought of him and his stubbornness. The bushes rustled faintly. From where she lay, she could see a clump of yucca in a fixed pattern against the sky. The voices by the fire became distant. The stars stooped near.

'In beauty it is begun. In beauty it is begun. Thanks.'

CHAPTER SIX

I

AT first light, before dawn, the desert is intimate, and each man feels the presence of others as intrusion. Blinding colour has not supplanted soft greys, uncertain forms; cliffs harsh by daylight, and thunderous-walled cañons loom soft with wells of coolness. The east is white—mother-of-pearl—the world is secret to each one's self.

Slim Girl, sitting apart, watching the slow increase of visible forms, looked towards the gambling hogahn. She heard them announce sunrise with the Magpie Song, and, after the last ringing 'It dawns, it dawns,' saw the straight dark forms coming out, moving away; some alone, some together talking, their voices intruding upon the hushed world.

She rose to intercept the path of one. He stood before her, answering her smile with a smile, tall and straight and shameless as he let his blanket fall to show—no silver belt, no jewelry, only the lucky bow-guard on his left wrist.

'Take this bow-guard, now, to keep. By first cold moon you will hear from me again. My uncles will look for you, or I shall.'

'So they won everything?'

'Everything.'

'Horse, belt, money?'

'Horse, belt, money. I go to T'o Tlakai to make silver.'

'You were foolish.'

'What else could I have done? And it was fine play!

49

I was happy. We made new songs about ourselves. Now I must work.'

She was prepared for this. 'You are not a man yet, I think.'

That gave him a start. 'Why do you say that? That is not a good thing to say.' Losing the goods meant little, but if losing them meant losing her, the world was a loom of lies.

'You are like a child. You are happy now, so you forget what you wanted before.'

'What thing?'

'Where is the love-song now? "Now my horse will not go From your valley, *a-a-a,*"' she sang.

'I tell you, I have nothing now. I have not even a horse. Nothing.' He struck his right hand across his left in emphatic gesture.

'I tell you, you do not have to pay for me. I have no mother. If you come, you must come now.'

'I am a man. I cannot come to you with nothing. I cannot let you buy me.'

'Look at me.' She shook herself so that her jewelry clanked. He heard the sound, but his eyes were upon hers. The east was banded with orange, red, and purple. 'Look at me.' Her eyes were long and narrow, and deep enough to absorb a man. 'I am rich. I shall give you silver and turquoise to work, horses to breed, till you too are rich. Must I tell you twice?' Her eyes were more beautiful than springs among the rocks. 'You have spoken to your uncle; you know what he said. Your mother will give you no sheep, no horses for me. If you want to come with me, come now. I cannot wait until first cold moon. You cannot cache me in a tree until you are ready for me. You have your manhood and your weapons; if you are not good enough with them, nothing can make you good enough. Come now.'

He was a long time answering, searching and searching her eyes. At last, 'It is good. Get your horse.'

She thought she had stood for twenty years with a rifle pointed at her breast. Her face did not change; she walked away slowly. He saw that full day lay golden along the tops of the cliffs, and the sky was brilliant; from the camps he heard the noise of departure, bustle and low voices and laughter that to an American would have seemed furtive.

I am like Natinesthani and the magician's daughter, he thought, but I have no sacred tobacco. I have just myself and my bow. I wonder what medicine will she give me? I shall make a bracelet that is like her walking; she is silver strong as iron. When I have horses again, we must both come back to T'o Tlakai. There is good water in Tseya Kien Cañon, that is the place for our hogahn.

He rolled a cigarette. The freshness would leave the air soon. Already he felt tired.

She rode as well as she danced or walked. Her pinto pony tossed it's head, working against her light touch on the reins, ringing the tinklers on its bridle. That girl on that horse—*ei-yei!* Reaching him, she smiled, and he forgot his fatigue. He walked tall and proud beside her, one hand on her stirrup, not caring who might see.

II

Red Man sought out Wounded Face where he stood at his pony's head, talking to Killed a Navajo. Despite a certain jauntiness, he did not look like a gambler who had just won a small fortune. He addressed the older man rather abruptly,

'Grandfather!'

'Yes?'

'Are you not the uncle of that man who won the horse-race, the one from T'o Tlakai?'

'I am. What is it?'

Red Man had meant to go slow, but his words were jumping out on him. 'Did he speak to you? Has he told you what he planned to do?'

Wounded Face and his friend suddenly lost all expression; they became wooden.

'I do not know what you mean. We talked together yesterday. What is in your mind?'

'He has gone to Chiziai. He has gone—he has gone—he has not gone alone.'

'He went with the woman who was stopped from dancing?'

'Yes.'

'Well?'

'Do you not know about her?'

'I have heard a little talk; I do not know anything. She is rich; perhaps it is a good marriage, I think.'

Red Man saw that Wounded Face very much wanted first-hand information. 'I live not far from Chiziai. I know, not just talk. She lives alone, she does no work, she is rich. The Americans make her rich, for badness. She is two faces and two tongues. You see her clothes and her skin, and hear her voice, but all the rest inside is American badness. I know. Hear me, I know.'

He had managed to be gay all night; he had been the cheerfullest of all the gamblers, the readiest singer, the pleasantest loser. Now suddenly it all went back on him. He moved his lips, and found he did not dare speak. He raised his hand to his mouth with two fingers outstretched, and thrust it forward—two-tongued. He struck his heart, then raised his fist before his face and brought it down rapidly—heart that kills with a knife. He struck his heart again, then brought his right fist down on his left hand—like a stone—making the gesture with all his force. He repeated how she made her living; in sign talk it was frightfully graphic and coarse.

'That is enough, Grandfather,' Wounded Face said. 'You did well to tell me.'

Red Man departed.

'Shall we ride after him?' Killed a Navajo asked.

'No. That is what that young man wants us to do, I think. You saw him, how moved he was. We have heard something of what he says, but still, he had reason to lie. Besides, it would be no use. He is like me, he is like his mother, and his father. You know them. When it is something serious he makes up his mind; you cannot move him unless you can convince him. I have six nephews, he is the best of them.' Wounded Face stood with his hand on his saddle, staring at the stirrup. 'Well, we can only wait. Do not speak of it, my friend.'

'I hear you.'

He mounted swiftly, and rode off at a trot.

III

It grew hot when the sun was halfway up. Laughing Boy's last sleep seemed years ago. From time to time he looked at her as one might drink at a spring, and her occasional speech was like rain falling. She rode in triumph.

Abruptly he stopped, gazing first at the trail, then over to the right, while with a hand on the bridle he stopped her horse. He said in a sure voice, 'Get off your horse.'

She did not quite know why she obeyed so immediately. He took off saddle and bridle, tied a thong about the animal's lower jaw, then stood for an instant, one hand on the withers, head raised high. She saw his lips moving, and was afraid of his intent face and a hard, excited look about his mouth. With a quick gesture he strung his bow, and before she could speak to him, mounted and was off, galloping. There was nothing for it but to wonder and wait.

She knew by the sun that he had not been gone over half an hour, but it seemed more than she could stand to wait longer. Her feelings alarmed her; was she falling in love? She saw him rounding a butte, trotting, driving two more ponies ahead of him. This, she thought, was madness. Truly, she must take him in hand. She rose as he drew near.

'What have you done? American Chief will put you in jail.'

'No; it is all right. That man'—he gestured toward the butte—'I did not hurt him much; besides, he is a Pah-Ute. He took this horse from my brother last year. He is bad, that one. He lives up beyond Oljeto. I saw him at the dance. Now I have something, to come with you. He was a bad shot, look.'

He showed her proudly a long, shallow scratch on his forearm.

'And the belt?' She pointed to the silver at his waist.

'I do not know from whom he stole that. It is a pretty good belt.'

They laughed together.

Immensely alone in that white stretch of adobe desert, they rode side by side, like two men, like friends. It seemed to Laughing Boy that she promised freedom and astonishing companionship; her small mannerisms, her casual remarks, were unconventional without consciousness; it was good. The ponies stepped out well despite the heat, the bridle jingled, the spare horse, with high head, pranced alongside, obedient to the rope. He sat slackly in the saddle, leaning back, flicking his pony's quarters in rhythm to his song.

They stopped seldom, ate little, and rode fast. It was hard on her; she was not accustomed to missing meals and sleeping where night happened to catch her, but she knew better than to complain. His easy toughness, his enjoyment of momentary comfort, were a compensation for her, and at night, camped beside a tiny waterhole, she listened to his singing.

She was tired and stiff. Already she had been alarmed, worried, tired, and hungry for this man. With a sudden fear, as she looked at him across the fire, she realized that she loved him. She had started something she could not stop, then. Well, it was all right, it was good. If only he hadn't gone off after that Pah-Ute, it wouldn't have happened; it was that waiting without understanding; it was that imperious warrior who gave her orders and was suddenly stronger than she, and apart from her. That had done it. While he sang, she looked at his hands locked across his knees, at the bowguard on his left wrist. When he loosed his shaft, the bowstring had snapped down across the leather on the inside; towards her he turned the lovingly worked silver on the back of it. The shaft had gone true, into the shoulder, between the neck and the butt of the aimed rifle. She shivered.

He stopped singing. She rose and sat down again close beside him, and waited. He made no move. She knew now that these next few days when she would be with him alone were desperately important to her, but she was meeting with a restraint blended of tribal custom and ignorance for which her knowledge of the American's world had not prepared her. It was beyond all other necessity to possess him fully now while the trail was single and straight, but he was a religious man, schooled to obedience of absolute conventions.

She thought. He was unused to her originality; she delighted him, but she came close at times to alarming him. She must go slow in all things. She would wait. The effort her decision cost her was so great that it frightened her. Perhaps, she told herself, it is a good

54

thing to have to wait. I love him, but I must remain mistress of myself and him. This is good for me.

She wanted to touch his face with her fingertips, to brush his hair with her lips. When they galloped together and he sang exultantly beside her, she wanted him to swing her to his saddle. There is very little gesture of tenderness in Indian experience, but she thought she saw latent in him the same desires, promising herself days to come when she would teach him many things. She thought to herself, I shall complete him with my knowledge. I shall make a god of him.

IV

The town of Los Palos shimmered in the heat. A lot of adobe houses and frame shacks pushed carelessly together were beaten down by the sun. Behind them was a strip of irrigated green like a back-drop, alfalfa, corn, beans, cottonwoods, a mile long and a few hundred yards wide. Rich, deep, cool green was not part of the desert landscape; it was something apart that the sands held prisoner. The mean little town was a parasite on the goodness of the water; here water and earth and man made beauty; there man and mud and boards created squalor.

A few yards of concrete and some blistered paint made a gesture of civic pride at the railroad's edge. A two-story hotel, compounding Spanish mission with cubism, was a monument of the railroad's profitable beneficence. From a rise where the trail crossed the railroad track, a little way to the west, it all compounded into a picture; the dejected town with its dominant hotel-station, the green strip behind it, yellow-grey sand, and farther, dancing buttes in the mirage.

Laughing Boy's attention was divided. 'Do these iron paths run all the way to Washindon? That is a beautiful place; there must be much water there. I have never seen so many houses; how many are there? Five hundred? I should like to go there. Are there many trading posts, or just one? Those are rich fields. Can one come here and see the iron-fire-drives?' He silenced himself, ashamed at having shown himself so carried away.

'Let us not go there now,' she told him quickly;

55

'it is better that we go first to my hogahn. The horses are tired.'

'You are right. Are there more than five hundred houses?'

'Yes, a few more. The iron-fire-drives goes by many times a day; it goes that way to Washindon and that way to Wide Water. Any one may see it. Come now.'

They gave the town a wide berth, trotting east past the end of the irrigated land along a trail between two buttes. About three miles farther on, where the clay walls widened again to face the southern desert, an adobe shack stood in the shadow of one wall. Behind it a tiny spring leaked out. Here they dismounted.

'But this is not a hogahn, it is a house. Did an American make it?'

'No, a Mexican built it. He went away to herd sheep, and I took it.'

He stepped inside. 'It does not smell like Mexicans.'

'I have been here a long time. Yellow Singer made the House Song for me. Is it not good? The door is to the east, like a hogahn.'

'Yes, it is good. It is better than a hogahn, I think; it is bigger and the rain will not come through. It will be good summer and winter.' He hobbled the horses. 'There is not much grass by that spring; we shall have to find pasture.'

'There is a little pasture just down there you can use. You must not let the horses run all over the place; this is American country. The Navajo country begins across the railroad track. There is good pasture just this side of Natahnetinn Mesa, enough for many horses. You must keep them up there.'

She lit a fire in front of the house.

'You have no loom. There is no sheep-pen.'

'I have been alone. I have had no one to weave for, and no sheep.'

'How do you live?'

She was laying the big logs over the first flame.

'I work a little bit, now and then, for the missionary's wife in the town. She is a good woman. Now I am going to set up a loom, and you shall have a forge.'

He thought that something was wrong. Her face was too blank. 'Not all missionaries are good, they

56

say. There used to be a bad one at T'o Nanasdési, they say.'

'No, not all of them are good; but this one is.' She spoke musingly. 'His wife pays me much money. She is not strong; I am.'

Her strange, pensive smile troubled him. He thought how beautiful she was. He thought again of the magician's daughter. He did not care what bad magic she might do to him; just she was worth all other things.

Sprawled out on his saddle-blanket, he watched as she brought food from the house and began to prepare it. Her movements were like grass in the wind. He eyed a banquet of luxury—canned goods, tomatoes, fruit.

'Perhaps when we go into the town to-morrow we can buy some candy.'

She thought, he must be kept away from town. I must think of something. 'I have a little here.'

'Sticks with stripes on them?'

'Yes.'

He sighed luxuriously. The food on the fire smelt good. It was cool. With a couple of ditches one could make a good cornfield by that spring, and plant peaches, perhaps. If they were to have food like this all the time— It was important to find that pasture for the horses, he must tend to it to-morrow. The town could wait. A swift movement caught his eye, lifting the coffee-pot aside. *Ei!* she was beautiful.

V

They talked as they ate, lounging, while night filled the valley.

'Do you speak American then?' Laughing Boy asked. 'Is it hard to learn?'

'It is not hard; we had to learn it. They put me in a room with a Ute girl and a Moqui and a Comanche; all we could do was learn English. Sometimes some Navajo girls sneaked out and talked together, but not often. They did not want us to be Indians.' She rested on her elbow, staring into the fire. 'They wanted us to be ashamed of being Indians. They wanted us to forget our mothers and fathers.'

'That is a bad thing. Why did they do that?'

'Do not talk about it. I do not want to think about those things.'

When she had put away the dishes, as they lit their cigarettes she said, 'If ever they come to take a child of ours to school, kill her.'

'Is it like that?'

'Yes.'

'I hear you.'

They lay side by side against the wall of the house, watching the fire. Her shoulder moved closer to him. He said,

'Tell me your true name.'

'My name is Came With War. What is yours?'

'My parents named me Sings Before Spears. It is a good name. Yours is good.'

'Why do they always give women names about war?'

'They have always done it. It brings good fortune to the whole People, I think.'

She moved so that she touched him. Sings Before Spears!

He asked her, 'Have you any relatives here? Some one must get a singer to make the prayers over us. There are the four days after that to wait; that is a long time. Let us have them end soon.'

She caught her breath and looked at him despairingly. He felt a wind blow between them while he met her eyes, a hollowness behind his heart. He clenched his left hand against his side, repeating slowly,

'Four days is a long time to wait,' and then almost inaudibly, 'Oh, beautiful!'

She looked away, wanting to laugh, to cry, to swear, and to kick him. He could not know; how could he know? She examined the line of his chin, the set of his lips, so very Indian in their fine chiselling and faint outthrust. Devices ran through her mind. This was a Navajo. This was something her missionaries and teachers never dreamed of. This was part of what she loved. She set her nails into the palms of her hands. Patience.

'I have a friend near here who will speak to a Singer to-morrow. He will be here to-morrow night.'

They smoked again. At last he said, 'I do not think

I shall sleep in your house now. I think it will be well to sleep up there.'

'Yes; that will be better.'

He got his blanket. 'I shall forget the trail.'

He loomed above her, in the play of darkness and firelight. She saw all the strength of the Navajo people embodied, against the sky, and she felt ashamed before it.

'Four days is not long, Laughing Boy.'

CHAPTER SEVEN

I

EARLY in the morning she got Laughing Boy off with the horses to find pasture. When he was well away, she put on American clothes; highlaced shoes, an outmoded, ill-fitting dress, high to the neck, long-sleeved, dowdy, the inevitable uniform of the school-trained Indian. It was a poor exchange for barbaric velveteen and calico, gay blanket and heavy silver. She had deleted from the formula a number of layers of underclothing; the slack, thin stuff indicated her breasts with curves and shadow; a breath of wind or a quick turn outlined firm stomach, round thigh, and supple movement, very little, but enough.

It began to be hot when she reached the wretched 'dobes and stick hovels on the outskirts of Los Palos, among the tin cans and the blowing dust. She stopped by a dome of sticks, old boxes, and bits of canvas.

'Hé, shichai!'

Yellow Singer crawled out into the sun, blinking red eyes.

'Hunh! What is it?'

His dirty turban had slipped over one ear, his hair was half undone. He sat looking at her uncertainly, his open mouth showing the remnants of yellow teeth. She noticed his toes coming out from the ends of cast-off army boots.

'Wake up. Were you drunk last night?'

He grinned. 'Very drunk. You lend me a dollar, perhaps?'

'You keep sober this morning, perhaps I give you a bottle.'

'Hunh?' He focussed his attention.

'I am going to be married this afternoon. I want you to come and sing over us.'

'Coyote!' He swore, and then in English, 'God damn! What do *you* want to get married for? What kind of a man have you caught?'

'You talk too much, I think; it may be bad for you some day. You come this afternoon and sing over us; I shall give you a bottle. Then you keep your mouth closed.'

He read her face, remembering that her grandmother had been an Apache who, in her time, had sat contemplating the antics of men tied on antheaps. And he knew this woman pretty well.

'Good, Grandmother,' he said respectfully, 'we shall come.'

She left without more words. In the town she had shopping to do—food, a jeweller's simple tools from a trader, a can of Velvet tobacco and big, brown Rumanian cigarette papers. Then she drifted idly to the post-office, sauntering past it in an abstracted manner, not seeing the men who lounged there. One of them immediately walked off in the other direction. She continued down the street, till it became merely a strip more worn than the land on either side of it at the edge of the town, where she entered a small, neat 'dobe house. In a few minutes he followed, closing the door behind him.

He wore a clean, checked woollen shirt, the usual big hat, and very worn, well-cut whipcord riding-breeches. He was of good height, light-haired but tanned, with rather sad eyes and a sensitive mouth. Even now, when he was plainly happy, one could see a certain unhappiness about him. He threw his hat on the table, put his hands on his hips, and drew a breath as he looked down on her, smiling.

'Well, you're back on time.'

'Yes why not? Didn't I tell you?' She held out her hand to him. Speaking English, she retained the Navajo intonation.

He sat down on the arm of her chair, and ran the tip of his index finger along the curve of her throat. 'That's a terrible dress, about the worst you've got. I'd like you to get some good clothes.'

'How will I do dat? Do you tink I can walk into dat store, dat one down dere, and dey sell me a dress? Will one of dose women, dey make dresses, work for me? You talk silly, you say dat. Maybe I give you my measure, maybe you write to dat place in Chicago, hey?'

'Sears Roebuck, my God! Well, it's not such a bad idea. All right, bring me your measurements.' He leant over to kiss her.

'Don't start dat now. I got to go back soon now.'

'What the hell?'

'My husban', he makes trouble, dat one. I can' stay away right now. Soon maybe.'

He heaved a sigh of exasperation. 'Listen! you've kept me waiting a week while you went off on that trip. Now you put me off again. You're always putting me off. I don't think you've got a husband.'

'Yes, I have, an' he's a long-hair. You know dat. Don't I point him out to you one time, dat one? You want him to kill me, hey?'

'Well, all right. To-morrow, then.'

'I can' do it. It ain't I don' want to, George. I can', dat's all.' She passed her hand along his cheek, slowly. 'You know dat.'

He kissed her finger-tips. 'Day after, then, Tuesday. That's flat, and no two ways about it. I have to go back to the ranch Wednesday; ought to be going back now. You can manage; I think you can manage anything you want. Understand? Tuesday.'

She studied him. He was difficult, this man. Now you had him, now you didn't. There were different kinds of Americans; this one came from the East; he was easy, and he was hard. Well, she could manage almost anything.

'All right, dat will be nice, I tink. I'll be glad to come den. So you go get me two bottle of wiskey now, to take home, den I fix it. Tuesday.'

'That old souse! I wish he'd fall over a cliff and break his damned neck.'

She smiled at him. 'I wish dat too, sometimes. but he ain't a bad man, dat one. He has been good for me.'

'I suppose so.'

'Now get de wiskey.'

'Kiss me first.'

II

She thought hard on the way home. The difficulties are beginning already. My path is beset with ambushes. And this is hard. Four days—Monday, Tuesday, Wednesday, Thursday, too late. Oh, no, Laughing Boy, I must bend you. I cannot be robbed of this, I have a right to it. Now I've got to manage, I, Came With War. I have earned this, I think. I am afraid of you, Sings Before Spears; I do not like to be afraid. I shall conquer you, or else I'll herd sheep. I cannot be conquered. God give me help—hmph, that God! Well, I know how. I make my own trail of beauty. I know what to do. I am strong, Laughing Boy, Laughing Boy.

She was dressed as a Navajo again when he returned from Natahnetinn. He inspected the jeweller's tools which she spread out for him, praising them, while she set to preparing food.

'They were talking about you in the town today,' she told him.

'How was that? I do not understand.'

'That Pah-Ute, the arrow went in farther than you thought. He went to Nahki Zhil trading post; there he bled to death. He told them about you. Now American Chief has made an order to put you in jail.'

'Perhaps we had better go away from here, then.'

'No, they will not do anything; it was only a Pah-Ute, they say. Only if you come into town and they see you, some policeman will take you then.'

'I am sorry. I should have liked to see that place. However, some day they may forget.'

'People have long memories for some things.'

Yellow Singer and his wife came just at the end of the afternoon. He watched them walking, with their long shadows rippling over the unevenness of the ground and the occasional bushes.

'What are those coming? They look like Pah-Utes, perhaps. They look like Hunger People! What rags!'

'They are Navajos; that is Yellow Singer. They look like that because they are poor, that's all. He has come to sing over us.'

There was something about those two faces that made Laughing Boy uncomfortable, as though a black veil had been pulled in front of them. They were people who would have unpleasant laughter. Both of them looked at him with open curiosity and an expression of understanding that bothered him. As they exchanged formal greetings, these two seemed to be extending to him a sympathy which he did not want. Then Slim Girl came out of the house dressed in her richest costume, and they were expressionless. Then, too, Laughing Boy was not concerned any more.

Yellow Singer's wife handed a medicine basket to Slim Girl, which she filled with the corn mush she had prepared. The singer placed it in the correct place on the floor of the house. Laughing Boy entered carefully. He was thinking hard about what he was doing; he was putting forth every effort to make it good and beautiful. He thought about the gods, about Slim Girl, about the future. It was all confused, because he was excited. He wished House God would come to stand over them; he thought Hunting Goddess would be a good one for her, or Young Goddess, or White Shell Woman. Now Yellow Singer's wife was leading her in. Under his breath, 'Oh, beautiful!'

She was thinking of many things at once; her excitement was deep down like a desert river under the sands. Now I really have a husband in my house. When this is over, it will be a test between us. I ought to feel all sorts of things, marrying like this now. You are handsome, Sings Before Spears. You do not know how much you are mine.

She sat down on the rug beside him. Yellow Singer divided the mush in four directions. Now he was praying for them. Laughing Boy concentrated his thought. Unreasonably, the girl was terrified lest something might happen. She was madly impatient. Now they partook of the yellow corn, ceremonially, and now it was Laughing Boy's turn to make a prayer. He sang the prayer to House God with solemn emphasis:

> 'House made of dawn light,
> House made of evening light,
> House made of dark cloud,
> House made of he-rain,
> House made of dark mist,
> House made of pollen . . .'

Yellow Singer's wife, fat and sleepy, sat in the corner. She was vaguely sorry for that young man. She rolled a cigarette, wishing he had not chosen so long a prayer.

> 'In beauty it is finished,
> In beauty it is finished.'

The confident, solemn voice ceased. He looked at Slim Girl. Now they were married 'in a beautiful way.' It might seem a little furtive, that ceremony without relatives, almost without guests, but now the gods had married them. Slim Girl was staring back at him with wide eyes.

Yellow Singer's wife stretched bulkily. 'Now let us feast.'

The old singer grinned. Slim Girl regarded them dreamily until her husband spoke to her,

'The guests must feast.'

She brought forth a banquet—canned tomatoes, pears, plums, beans, candies, pop, white bread. She heated the coffee, and set it out with plenty of sugar, and cups for all. On one side she put down a bottle of what looked like water.

'It is a feast,' said Yellow Singer.

They all started eating. The old man took some of the clear liquid, and passed it to his wife, who drank and offered it to Laughing Boy.

'What is it?'

'Whiskey,' Slim Girl spoke quickly; 'he does not know how to drink it.'

'I should like to try it.'

'It is good; you should take it, Grandfather. We all like it.' Yellow Singer chuckled.

'I do not think he can stand it,' Slim Girl said thoughtfully.

'Let me try it. It is right that I should find out about these things. Give me the bottle.'

He saw that her eyes, watching him, were speculative, with something hidden in back of them. He thought she was measuring him.

'Give it to me.'

'Wait. You are not used to it; let me fix it for you. I can make it taste good.'

She took out an orange and a lemon, that she had had hidden behind the water jar.

'What are those?'

'That is called "lanch." This yellow one is "lemon"; there is no word for it in Navajo. They are American fruits; they grow on trees, like peaches.'

She made a stiffish drink in a tin cup, sweetened with a great deal of sugar.

'You never did that for me,' Yellow Singer muttered to his wife.

'I shall do it for you, that thing—when you are as young and handsome as he is.'

They watched him with grinning interest while he tried the drink. Slim Girl was inattentive.

'But this is good! This is better than that red boiling water, I think.' He nodded towards his bottle of pop. It began to glow in his stomach. 'What is it doing to me?'

'It is beginning to do its good, little brother.' The medicine man pulled at the bottle in sympathy. 'By and by you will love it, that feeling.' His wife reached for her share.

Slim Girl stood up. 'The sun is setting. If you take much more of that now, you will not find your way home. Here is a bottle for you to take with you.'

Inside the house it was half dark, and the doorway framed the clay bluffs opposite, painted with sunset. She rearranged the blankets and sheepskins for reclining against the wall, and there relaxed, smoking a cigarette.

He finished his drink, liking the flavoured sugar in the bottom of it.

'Sit over here, and let us talk a little now.'

He placed himself half-sitting, half-lying beside her.

'That is queer, that drink. I feel queer here,' touching the hinge of his jaw, 'as if something were squeezing my teeth. But it is good; make me some more of it.'

'Not right away.'

'It would be good to sing, I think. Let us sing some very beautiful prayers together. Everything is good now.'

'Let us just think for a little bit, now we are married.'

'Now we are married. Why are you looking at me like that? I do not understand you all the time, what your face means.'

'I like to look at you, Sings Before Spears.' Her hand fell into his, he felt her beside him. Something told him that that was only half an answer. He touched her face with his finger-tips. She was studying him intently.

Then she kissed him. He did not understand it; her face suddenly near his, against his, distorted so close to his eyes, her eyes run together. He was held tightly, and something wet, at once hot and cool was against his mouth, with a tiny, fierce imprint of teeth. Vaguely he remembered hearing that Americans did this. He did not understand it; he had a feeling of messiness and disgust. He tried to move away, but she held him; he was pressed against the wall and the sheepskins. She was fastened onto him; he could feel all her body, it was entering into him. There was something uncontrolled, indecent about this. Everything became confused. A little flame ran along his veins. The world melted away from under him, his body became water floating in air, all his life was in his lips, mouth to mouth and breath against his face. He shut his eyes. His arms were around her. Now, almost unwittingly, he began to return her kisses.

III

Slim Girl was asleep. Laughing Boy was very tired, but there was no rest for him. It was black inside the house; here no night wind blew through the leaves of the hogahn wall, no stars looked down through a smoke-hole. He found his tobacco and stole outside.

The cold night wind blew against his skin. His eyes rested among the shadowy forms of the buttes; he looked up at the thick-gathered, cool stars. It was like laying a cold knife-blade against a burnt finger. It was right that they gave women names about war; he understood that now.

His feet took him up onto the high place above the spring, where he had slept before. There he made himself comfortable with his back against a piñon trunk, smoking. Everything was whirling within him: it was necessary to put his thoughts in order. He had never imagined it was anything like this. He had lived the intimate life of the *hogahn,* he knew the camp-fire jokes; but there was never a hint of this kind of thing. It might be just American tricks, but he thought not. No, it was she, her power. She was stronger than iron or fire. That drink was medicine, but she was not medicine; it was just she herself. That blade of grass of a girl, that little Slim Girl, she could make his belly turn over inside of him, she could make his interior dissolve. He sat wondering at her and at himself. So very uncontrolled, at moments he felt ashamed, but mostly it was wonder. That girl was like one of the Divine People. One should not forget one's self, but this was a beautiful thing.

He had fought, and sung, and raced horses, and known the uplift of the great dances; he was old friends with hunger, cold, fatigue, and suddenly contrasted feasting and comfort; he had lived out to the tips of his fingers, but this was something that made everything else turn thin and shadowy. That was her magic, perhaps, and it was wonderful, it altered life: that she gave complete fulfilment, where everything else was partial. Her house was better than other Indians' houses, her food was richer than other Indians ate, and she fed one's spirit with a perfection that only she could give. Hunger was dead where she was. She was not like The People; life with her would have to be different, but the trail was beautiful.

His cigarette was long dead. Boy Chasing His Arrow had moved far across the sky. Drowsiness mingled itself with his thoughts, blurring them, while the night wind blew upon him. His doubts and wonderments faded and thickened into sleep. Sleeping, he dreamed a dream. Perhaps the sight of the ragged, wretched singer and his wife had put it into his head. It was not much of a dream, not elaborate.

He sat by the hogahn fire, and his uncle was telling the end of the Coming Up Story. He did not really see much, but he knew it was his uncle, and he felt angry with him for what he had said about Slim Girl. He knew that the other children were there, and that the snow coming through the smoke-hole melted in the air, and fell on the fire with little hisses. It was his uncle speaking, it was Wind God speaking in his mind; they were the same. None of that was clear; only the old, familiar words came to him, very definitely, spoken with emphasis, as when one wants to impress a lesson upon children.

'Slayer of Enemy Gods came to the Hunger People, they say . . . He said, "Now I am going to kill you, because you are bad for my people." Hunger Chief said, "If you kill us, nobody will be hungry any more, nobody will care about feasting. They will not go out and hunt for good food, venison, and fat prairie-dog. Nobody will want to go hunting," he said, they say.

'Slayer of Enemy Gods said, "Then I shall let you live," they say.'

He heard Talking God call in the distance, 'Wu, wu, wu, wu!' Then the god called again, nearer. He knew he was asleep, and tried to wake, to meet the god coming. He was terrified lest he should be asleep when the god called for the fourth time. He had an idea that he had put himself asleep deliberately, against the god's will. The call sounded for a third time, just outside the hogahn. Talking God was out there, standing on a bent rainbow, in company with many other Divine Ones. He had shut himself up in a pitchblack place with no entrance; he had locked himself away from the gods under a blanket of dark clouds.

With a desperate effort he woke, sitting up, gasping with relief. His eyes drank in the dawn, the open space, the tree, the clay buttes, things apart from his dream. Over across, a turtle-dove called, 'Hoo, hoo, hoo-hoo-hoo.'

CHAPTER EIGHT

I

She was still asleep inside the house. He stood looking down upon her in the half-light. She seemed frail, childish, and sweet, with the shadow under the eyelids, her mouth faintly drooping, her figure reduced to almost nothing beneath the blanket. He thought of that drama of strength and weakness, of conquering and being conquered, fitting it to this small person, soft in sleep. Now that he was looking at her, he had no reservations; it only seemed a miracle that she should be his. He wondered at the mere chance it was; Slender Hair speaking to him of the dance and the racing, coming to Tsé Lani, this little incident and that, until out of nowhere that which might never have been entered and became the core of his life.

The sun would be up soon. He wen tto meet it.

'Dawn Boy, little chief,
May all be beautiful before me as I wander . . .'

She woke happy, watching him under lazy eyelids as he stood outside the door, naked save for his breech-clout, with the level sunlight touching the edges of his flanks and ribs, making a golden reflection where his upraised arms bunched the muscles at his shoulders. She thanked God and the gods indiscriminately. Whatever happened now, this could not be taken away. She shifted the blanket, closed her eyes, and assumed sleep.

He sat down beside her, a little nervous about her a-wakening. Her eyelids quivered, she yawned deliciously, she stretched her arms like a kitten playing. She sat up and smiled at him, seeing his face brighten as he responded.

'Have I slept so late? I shall get your breakfast as soon as I have fixed your hair. You should see it.'

He felt of its disarray, with the queue hanging lopsided, then he grinned at her. 'Your own is just as bad; go look at yourself in the spring.'

She reached over to a shelf and took down a small mirror, which she handed to him. He looked at himself in it: this was fascinating but a little disappointing. Finally she took it from him.

'Come, now, dress, and do up my hair.'

He had often exchanged that service with his brothers and sisters; it was a pleasant and friendly act. He had watched his mother and father together at it, one leaning against the other's knees, laughing when the brush pulled too hard, and he had seen that they extracted some pleasure from it which he did not know. Now he understood that, and the sheer domesticity of it delighted him. He felt really married, settled, a man who would soon have children, and speak as one of established position, no more a boy.

'To-day you must get me the wood for a loom,' she told him. 'It is a long time since I have woven, but I have beautiful blankets in my mind. I shall weave and you shall make jewelry.'

'No, to-day, before we do anything, we must make a sweat-bath. This is all different, here. We are starting off new. We must make ourselves clean, we must make a fresh start. And, besides, how can you weave? You have no sheep.'

'I shall buy wool in the store in town. They sell good wool there; the people round here bring it in.'

'Why do we not raise sheep? I have some in my mother's flock I could get.'

'Who will keep them? You will have your horses and your jewelry; that will be plenty. I must always be going in to work for that missionary woman.'

'I do not like your working in there.'

'Why, have you some bad thought?'

'Why, I have no bad thought. But a house is empty when the woman is away.'

'I used to work for her every day; now I only work sometimes. She gives me good money. It is because of her that you will have silver to work with. To-morrow, when I go in, I shall bring you Mexican silver. And those days you can go tend to the horses. By and by, when we have made much money with your jewelry and horses and my weaving and work, we shall go back to your country. We shall go back rich. Is it not a good plan?'

'You have spoken well. Here, I do not know about these things, but you know, and your words are good. It is enough for me that I have you. It is not just that we are married, but we are married all through; there is not any part of us left out.'

'No; there is not any part of us left out. And you do not want a second wife, Laughing Boy?'

'No—no!' The extra-emphatic, three syllable negative, *'E-do-ta!'* long-drawn-out, with the decisive sign of the right hand sweeping away. 'Have you a sister you want me to take? If you want help here, in the hogahn, I will get one, but she will not be for me. She will be in the way. You are enough for me; perhaps you are too much for me, I think.'

Quickly she kissed him. He felt embarrassed, and loved it.

He had to teach her the ritual and song of purification, but, with faint childhood memories to aid her, she was quick to learn. Her close attention pleased him, and it was a pleasure to hear her sing. He was only sorry for her, that she had for so long been denied these things, and angry and puzzled at the schools and the American life that had forbidden them. In the end, he taught her songs that she had no business knowing, quite aware of what he did, as a kind of unavowed tribute and token of the special quality he felt in her.

II

After the steam bath and the water and the foaming yucca-suds, it was good to lie with hair spread out, drying, and talk vaguely of things to be done, and now and again to touch her. Great achievements completed themselves in a phrase. He drew the design of a bracelet in the sand; he braided his hair and mimicked the nasal

71

speech of a Ute. They fell to talking of the ways of different tribes, the old wars, and the present semi-hostility between the Navajo and the Pah-Utes.

'There is not often trouble with them,' he told her 'but we do not like them. They live wild up in that country beyond Oljeto, where they are hard to catch, and they steal things. Mostly they trouble the Mormons; the Mormons are afraid of them, they say. Since I was a little boy, only once we had real trouble with them. Then one time we went on the war-path for them. I went on the war-path that time.'

He felt proud of the part he had played, and wanted to tell her about it.

'That was three years ago; I was just about full grown. Blunt Nose, he made the trouble, that one. He was chief of a band of them; he lived up beyond Naesjé Cañon, near Tsé Nanaazh. That is wild country, almost in the mountains. He was bad.

'He used to kill Mormon cattle all the time, a cow, and a cow, and a cow, here and there. He needed to keep no sheep. He did the way he pleased. He wore two pistols, and had a gun on his saddle, they say. He would ride down the middle of the trail, and not turn out for any one.

'One time he heard the Mormons had sent for soldiers, so he left their country alone. Then he sat quiet for a while, but his people got hungry. A Pah-Ute will eat almost anything, but there is very little up there. That is why the Navajos leave them alone; there is nothing in that country but a few Pah-Utes and a few antelopes. You cannot make anything out of the skins of either, so we let them alone.

'Well, now Blunt Nose decided to try mutton. He came down by Jahai Spring where Hungry Man lived. He had all his braves with him. They started to run off Hungry Man's sheep. Then The Doer came along. You have heard of him? He is the one who killed those two Americans; his father was Generous Chief, the one who never was captured when The People went into exile. So The Doer came along; he saw that man's wife, where she came running. He rode up, he started shooting at those men. They shot back at him. They were too many for him; he rode away and they chased him. But he killed one.

'Then Blunt Nose was angry. He killed Hungry Man, and his two children. He ran off the sheep. He went back into the Naesjé country.

'The People around there gathered together to hunt him, but the trader at Oljeto told them not to. He told them to wait while he wrote a paper to American Chief at T'o Nanasdési. So they did that. Meantime Blunt Nose was talking. He learned that there were no soldiers in the Mormon country, but he said he liked mutton. He said no Coyote could kill one of his braves and not be punished; he said the Coyote People would pay for what they had done. He talked like this all around; he talked brave, calling us that name.

'In a little while he came down again. But they had men on watch, they made smoke signals. A lot of people came together and went after him, so that he had to make a big circle, around by Oljeto, to get back. When he went past the trading post, he shot into it. He did not hurt any one, but he spoiled some tin cans and broke some windows. Then, on his way home, he crossed the bridge over T'o Atsisi Creek. It is a big wooden bridge that you can ride a horse over; Washindon had it built. They sent two Americans to show how it should be built.

'Well, he came by this bridge. He was angry, so he burnt it, that man. And he got some sheep, and went home.

'Then the trader wrote another paper, a strong one, and sent it to American Chief. Meantime The Doer was getting up a war-party. The People were angry; they wanted to kill them, all those Pah-Utes. So American Chief wrote a paper saying that he was getting up a war-party of Americans who would do the fighting. He said to have good horses ready for them, and that the Navajos must not start fighting or there would be soldiers. That was what he said.

'He tried to talk to Dokoslid over the talking wires, to get the war-party, but a man down by Besh Nanaazh had cut some of the wires to mend his wagon, so he had to wait a day to fix them. Meantime he sent a rider with this paper.

'The rider came by Gomulli T'o trading post. His horse was lame and he was tired. I was there with a good horse, a roan. Yellow Mustache was the trader there; he told me to carry the paper. He told me to ride hard. He said I would be paid.

'I rode all day. I rode at night until the moon set. I rode after it was all dark, but I was afraid of the spirits. Then I made camp. The next morning I saw a fresh horse, so I caught it and rode on. The sun was about halfway up when I saw Oljeto. And right then the Pah-Utes saw me. They started after me, and I went as hard as I could for the trading post.

'I could hear them shooting at me; I could hear their bullets. I was very much afraid, but there was nothing to do except ride hard.

'Then I felt something hit me. It made a dull thump; it did not hurt. I thought, "I have been hit in the bottom of my spine. In a minute it will hurt. Probably I shall die. I do not want to die." That way I thought.

'I thought all that all at once, then I felt behind, but there was nothing. Then people began shooting from the windows of the trading post, and the Pah-Utes went away. I rode up to the door and got off, wondering if I should fall. But I was all right. There was a bullet in the cantle of my saddle; that was what I had felt.

'We waited five days for the American war-party; meantime they got some good horses together. Blunt Nose was around all the time. People gathered together in groups of ten to twelve families, or more, like in the days when we were always at war. Then those men came.

'There were eight of them. They all had badges on their shirts, like policemen, only not quite the same. One of them was a fat man; we did not see why they brought him.

'They said they wanted four Navajos to be trackers. The Doer was to be head tracker. There were two other young men, and then they took me. They said they would pay me a dollar a day. That was a new idea to me, to be paid for hunting Pah-Utes. I thought you just hunted them.

'We tracked them for three days without seeing them. They tried to make us go at night, but we pretended not to be able to follow the trail. When The Doer told them that, they believed him. It was not an easy trail. Their

74

horses were not shod, and they went a great deal over bald rock, they turned and doubled, they dragged branches behind them.

'We did not get much to eat, we could not make a fire. Those Americans brought a brown, sweet candy, and a little, dried-up black candy in boxes, something sticky. These we ate; you could go a long time on them. Then we had some dried corn. We started at first light; we went till it was quite dark. During the day it was hot among those rocks. We were hungry. It did not seem that we were following Pah-Utes; we were just following tracks in the sand, or little scratches on the rock, and some day we should come to the end of them, and something important would happen. Now the only thing in the world was those marks. When you saw one where you had not expected it, it seemed to shout at you.

'But we were gaining on them. On the fourth day they were much fresher, those tracks. We were close to them. Then we saw a couple of them, on lame horses, and we chased them. They had to cross a deep arroyo; when they went down into it we raced, hoping to catch them at the bottom of it. But they got up the other side; they just came up that side when we got on the near edge. Right away they started shooting. They shot at that fat man.

'Right away he fell off the horse. He landed on his stomach, and as soon as he landed he began to shoot. He shot between his horse's legs. He hit one Pah-Ute in the leg and one in the arm. Then we knew why he had been brought along, that fat man.

'We wanted to kill them, but the chief American said that they had to go to T'o Nanasdési to be punished. Their horses were no good, so they put them on those two young men's horses, and sent them back with them and one American to Oljeto. That left me and The Doer. I had never seen him before, that man, but everybody has heard about him. I was anxious to do well in his eyes.

'In the afternoon we came to the mouth of Yotatséyi Cañon. The trail was fresh and clear. The Doer told them that the other end of the cañon was halfway up Napani Mountain, to our right. It went in a big curve, he said. If they got out there, we could never catch them, he said. So he told them to send three men with him, and he would take them straight across there. He would reach it by nightfall, he said. Then, in the morning, we could start in from both ends and catch them, he said. So they did that. I stayed with the four at the lower end. I thought about there being still ten Pah-Utes, but I did not say anything. I did not want to seem afraid, if The Doer was not.

'We went a little way into the cañon and made camp. The chief American lent me a pair of magic tubes that he had, that you put to your eyes, and they made everything far away look near. I watched with them until I saw The Doer's smoke signals. He signalled that they had had a fight, and the enemy were coming towards us. So we watched, but we saw no sign of them. It was dark soon after. We watched all night.

'When it was getting near dawn, but no light as yet, we started on foot. As soon as there was a little light, they sent me along the top of the talus along one wall, to look out for ambushes. The cañon was about five hundred paces wide; the walls were at least that high. The chief American watched me with those tubes. I would wave my hand, as a sign that I saw no one, and they would come foward, strung out across the cañon.

'It was full light when we got near where the cañon turned the corner. I went on ahead again, very slowly. I could look down into the sand and see the tracks that we had been following so long. I felt very much alone. I knew that man was watching me as I crept; that made me feel a little better. My father told me that the war-path was like stalking mountain sheep, only more exciting. I thought that there was more to it than that. Mountain sheep do not shoot back at you: mountain sheep are not people who are thinking about you just as hard as you are thinking about them.

'Then I saw them. They must have made camp up in the middle of Yotatséyi; now they were coming to try to get out this way. There were nine of them, in single file, riding carefully and watching. So I signalled to the Americans, and saw them take cover. I made myself as hard to see as I could. Suddenly I thought that I was enjoying myself a great deal.

'They came around the corner; now I looked right down on them, from behind a bush. One of them, looking around, looked straight at my bush. He was searching for people hiding. I thought that that bush was not nearly thick enough. His eyes passed on, and for just a moment I felt weak.

'Then the Americans started shooting. So I stood up and gave the war-cry and started. As I was shouting, I thought, they will hear the Coyote howl and know he's a Wolf. There was a brave just below me in a buckskin shirt with beadwork on it, and a hat with a silver hatband. I noticed all about him while I shot at him. I wanted it to be known that I had killed one. I saw my arrow in the air a long time; I saw it strike. He fell off his horse. Then I saw that he was not dead, and I was glad. I do not know why.

'There were five of them down now, and the others put up their hands, so the Americans took them prisoners. One had been killed over in the other end of the cañon.

'We went back to Oljeto, and they paid us as they said. Then we had ourselves purified from the blood, and we spent several dollars on canned food. I bought a big paper bag, as big as a hat, full of all different kinds of candy, and went home, and we all ate it.

'When I was telling about what happened, I got to the part about thinking I was shot, and I started to laugh. I could not stop, I just laughed. So they started calling me by that name. That is all.'

Slim Girl said, 'I am glad you are a man like that.' She thought to herself, he is a warrior. That was worth ten thousand schools. He must have been about eighteen. Where is basketball against that?

III

Before supper there was the well-mixed drink again, with its attendant elation and the curious feeling at the back of his teeth. He finished the brew.

'I should like to take some more of that.'

'That is not a good thing to do.'

'Why not?'

'If you take too much you become foolish. You grow old before your time.'

'That would not be good. Perhaps it would be better not to take any. You do not take it.'

'It is not every one who is able to drink it. It is not meant for women, that drink, it is for men. If I take it, it makes me sick quickly. It is all right for you, you are strong. It just makes you feel well, doesn't it? You like it, I think?'

'Yes, I like it. I think it is good for me.'

'It is good for you.' And she told herself, 'I shall tie you with it. It is another hobble around your feet, so that you will not go away from me.'

CHAPTER NINE

I

TIME passing and corn growing cannot be seen; one can notice only that the moon has become so much older, the corn so much higher. With a new life almost more regular than the old, yet far more thrilling, with a rich supply of silver and choice turquoise, with horses to trade and a cornfield to care for, and all the world made over new, time for Laughing Boy went like a swift, quiet river under cottonwood trees. For him, life—which had never been a problem—was solved and perfected, with none of Slim Girl's complication of feeling that such happiness was too good to last. Had he sat down at T'o Tlakai to compose a song of perfection, he could not have imagined anything approaching this.

It had always been a pleasure to him to work in the corn, to help make the green shafts shoot up, to watch them dance, and contrast their deep, full green with the harsh, faded desert. Among his people corn was a living thing; to make a field beautiful was not so far from making a fine bracelet, and far more useful. He drew the precious water into his field thriftily. At its corners he planted the four sacred plants.

Slim Girl did not understand it at first; she had rather wanted to bar it as entailing unnecessary labour, but decided not to say anything. He saw that she thought it dull, drudging work. He did not try to explain it to her directly, but told her the story of Natinesthani and the origin of corn, and taught her the songs about the tall plant growing. When the stalks were past waist-high, he took her to the field at evening, while sunset brought the drab clay bluffs to life with red, and a soft breeze made the leaves swing and whisper. He made her see the individual hills, the slender plants and their promise, talking to her of Corn Maiden and Pollen Boy, and of how First Man and First Woman were made from corn. Her eyes were opened to it then, as much through understanding how he felt as through what she objectively beheld. After that she worked with him a little, to please him, although she never cared for the back-breaking toil in itself.

His silver sold well. His craftsmanship was fine, his invention lively, and his taste in turquoise most exacting. It was strong, pure stuff, real Northern Navajo work, untouched by European influence. Other Indians would buy it in the store, and its barbaric quality caught the tourist's eye. Slim Girl got in touch with the Harvey agent, finding him a ready buyer at good prices. She liked to think, then, of the many places along the railroad in which strangers were paying for her husband's work.

She had learned not to care much for general opinion of herself, and was surprised to find that this tangible evidence of her mythical husband's existence, this visible means of support, made a pleasant difference in the trader's attitude towards her, and eventually in the looks she received from men throughout the town. There was a surprised feeling that she must have been telling the truth about herself, and a grateful decrease in attempts to scrape unwelcome acquaintance with her. As for George Hartshorn, her American, he developed an increased jealousy that she knew how to use.

To complete her idyll, she wanted to weave, and she found it harder than she had expected. She had been taken to school young, before she had become skilled, and now it was almost all forgotten. Laughing Boy even had to teach her the names of her tools. She wondered, as he watched her struggling with the stubborn warp, if he were laughing at her inside himself, if she seemed ridiculous to him. Many times she would have given up had it not been for her natural determination of character, and for knowing how anomalous and incomplete to him was the house in which the woman could not make a blanket. She dearly longed to reconstruct that scene, but after just a little her back would ache, her forearms grow heavy, and in the backs of her hands would be sharp pains, while the threads were like demons to outwit her. The patient, monotonous spinning was pure torture, and she knew little or nothing of dyes.

Of course, her first blanket was an ambitious one, elaborately designed. The conception was simplified in the making, and the finished product was a quarter of the originally intended size. When she cut the sorry object from the loom, and looked at it, all crooked, irregular, and full of holes, she could have cried. She hid it from him. Many of her later attempts, not fit to go under a saddle or be sold, she destroyed, but this was the first thing she had made. It was a sad failure, but she could see what it was meant to be, and she kept it.

She wove perfectly plain strips that might serve to be sat on, and even many of these were hopeless. At times, despite her husband's encouragement, in his absence she would curse fluently in English and yank at the strings. Few things could make her lose control of herself thus; she wondered at herself for continuing. It was an offering to her beloved and, unconsciously, an expiation for a guilt she had not admitted.

II

On a day when the corn was nearly ripe, she went to work in the field. Tiring, she sat down to rest where she could watch two stalks, with their silk just showing against the sky. Low on the horizon the beginnings of a storm darkened the blue. She called Laughing Boy.

'Show me how they draw the corn in the sand-pictures.'

'I do not think I should show you that. You are a woman, and you have never seen the true gods in the Night Chant.'

'Perhaps you are right.'

He was making a decision.

'I shall show you.' He drew in the sand. 'We do it like this. Here is blue, here yellow. Here are the tassels, the silk.'

'Why do you show me?'

'You are not like ordinary people, you have a strength of your own. I do not think any harm will come to you.'

She looked from the conventionalization to the growing stalks; she divided the threatening sky into a design. Her first, elaborate blanket had been a built-up, borrowed idea, her later ones were uninteresting accidents. Now she saw her work complete, loving it and the task of making it. Now she really had something to tell her loom.

She was impatiently patient with the dyeing and spinning, needlessly afraid that she would lose her inspiration. When she was ready, she worked so steadily that Laughing Boy warned her of the fate of women who wove too much, and forced her to let a day go by. Her muscles were much tougher now, and her fingers had grown clever and hard among the strands.

She managed for him to be away with his horses during the last two days, when she finished it. He had not yet returned when, a little despondently, she locked in the selvage, unrolled it on the frame, and sat back on her heels to smoke and look. She did not see what she had conceived. She did not see a living design, balanced and simple, with mated colours. She saw thin, messy workmanship, irregular lines, blunders, coarsenesses. At one place she had forgotten to lock the blue into the green weft, sunlight showed through. The counting of stitches was uneven. The blanket was not even a rectangle.

81

She went quickly away from the house, walking hurriedly and smoking fiercely.

'I am not a Navajo; it is not given to me to do these things. Mother was happy when she wove, she was beautiful then. I cannot make anything, and he is gifted. He will despise me in the end. Being able to make something beautiful is important to him. He will feel his house empty without the sound of weaving. They said I was gifted, that man who came that time. "My child, just stick to the things of your people and you will do something. You have it." "Mr. Waters is a very famous artist, you must pay attention to what he says, my dear. He expressed himself much pleased with your pictures. I am sure the whole class is proud of Lillian to-day." Those crayons were easy. Perhaps he would like that. But I want to weave. There is nothing the matter with me. No use. *God damn it to hell! God damn me! Chindi, mai, shash, Jee-Cri!* Well, let's go and look at it. There's his pony in front of the house. Come on.'

He had taken down the blanket and was pegging it out carefully. All he said was,

'Where are your wool cards?'

She brought them, two implements like very sharp curry-combs, used to prepare the wool for spinning. She sat down to watch him, thinking, 'Perhaps I shall get very drunk. That might help.'

He carded the face of the blanket energetically, so roughly that it seemed a gratuitous insult even to her poor work. The very coarseness of her spinning served his purpose, as the sharp teeth scraped and tore across the design. She wondered if he were trying to efface it. He stood up.

'Now come here and look.' He put his arm over her shoulder. 'You have thought well. The picture is beautiful.'

The scraping had torn loose a long wool nap, almost a fur, fluffy and fine, that covered all the errors of the weaving. The sharp edges were lost, but the lovely combination she had dreamed of was there, soft and blurred, as though one saw it through tears. She could see how good her conception had been, how true and sure. She had made a beautiful thing. She looked and looked.

He loosened the pegs and turned up the untouched side. As he turned it, he jerked at the corners, throwing the uncertain weave out of shape. It looked like a child's work.

'I am not telling you a lot of things. I am just letting you see something. I think you understand it.'

'I understand. You will be able to put my next blanket under your saddle, and be proud of it. Thank you.'

III

After that there were long, flawless days when they were at home together, he at his forge, she at her loom, time passing with the thump of the batten, the ring of the hammer or rasp of the file. There were chatter and laughter, songs, and long, rich silences. Work then was all love and inspiration.

She had known a good many different kinds of pleasure, but this was a new richness, something that did not exhaust itself, but grew, a sharing of achievement, designs, colours; fingers, hands, and brain creating, overcoming. There was the talk and hummed songs. There was a great deal to be silent about. It came to her as she was weaving the coloured threads to her intent, Why was this not enough?

This is it. This is the thing I have always wanted. There is nothing better; why endanger it. Why not let that man go now? Why not just do this?

The batten thumping down on the weft, the hammer ringing on white metal.

As long as I keep on my way, there is danger. I could never go back to what used to be now. This is what is worth while. A hogahn in the Northern desert would be beautiful now.

Sure fingers interlocking dark blue and black, driving the toothed stick down over the juncture.

I cannot stop halfway now. I am making a new trail of beauty. When I get through, it will be wonderful. Nothing will ever have been like our life.

Lifting the treadle to let a line of crimson follow the shuttle through the design.

We shall command money, money will command

83

everything. I have herded sheep, their dust in their lungs, hot, a little girl howling at the sheep. We shall be above that. *Aigisi hogahn hojoni*. A little girl watching old Light Man drive by to his summer camp in a buckboard behind two spanking pintos.

A tiny touch of white brings the red meander to life, and deepens the thunderous background.

Navajo women are growing old when Americans are just getting really strong. I am not going to turn into a fat old squaw. My dear, my dear, will you be gay when you are old? Your silver is beautiful. Is anything in the world worth the risk of separating your forge and my loom?

The blue shuttle goes under six warp strands, the black, coming under two, meets it. A close weave looks like a true diagonal.

Are you afraid now, Came With War? I can handle these men. I make my own trail, and I do not stop halfway. I shall make something perfect, that nobody else has made. If I stop now, I might as well stop work on this blanket, after all it cost me to learn to make it. I shall pay myself back for everything that has been.

A single weft strand has no thickness at all, and a blanket is long. It needs patience to finish it, and to make it beautiful, one must not be afraid of the colours.

Laughing Boy, having done his thinking and made up his mind, did not mull over his decision, any more than when he had started a bracelet; he worried whether it ought to have been a necklace. If he did think of other forms, it was only in reflecting that after this was done he would make more, and always more.

You make your dies out of iron files, you get some small piece of iron from a trader for your anvil. In a hard wooden board you cut depressions for hammering out bosses and conchos and hemispheres for beads. When you have bought or made your tools, and have your skill, you go ahead. You make many things, rings, bracelets, bow-guards, necklaces, pendants, belts, bridles, buttons, hatbands. No two are alike, but they are all of the silver and turquoise.

Having what he had, he went ahead with living. There were many days, all different, some of high emotion, some of mere happiness, but they were all made of the same stuff; there was one element beautified in all of them. So he worked, content.

When he had made something that had truly satisfied him, he would give it to her, saying, 'That is for you. There is no use selling that to Americans, they do not understand.'

It always pleased her, but she would appraise the jewelry carefully, checking it against their mutual profits, his sales and horse trades, her blankets, and what she brought from the town. If it could be paid for, she put it away, otherwise she required that it be earned. Her primitive banking won his astonished admiration. For her, it was a happy symbol that their fortune, however earned, should be stored in things of beauty.

And every day, at the end, the sun went down and the harsh horizons dimmed. Then there was the magic drink ready for him, and after that a banquet. They spoke dreamily in the firelight, side by side, and knew a great intimacy. They were not two individuals, but two parts who together made a whole, and there was no cleavage between them.

CHAPTER TEN

I

THE first time Laughing Boy rode away to Natahnetinn with the horses, he rebelled against the need to leave their tiny valley, and against the prospect of recurring trips, some of several days' duration. But very shortly he found that, no matter how much in love, a man needs both time to himself, alone, and in general periods of being away from the sphere which is permeated by the influence of a woman. He had a use for these days alone. After all, at the end of a day the sun always set, and it was less than half the time that a strayed animal, a bit of trading or the need of moving his herd kept him away overnight.

Here he could ride the range and sing. Here it was that he thought of the best designs for his silver. It was beautiful, too, watching the long-maned ponies in the good grass, or coming down to water. Then there was the trading, meat and drink to a Navajo—patience, bluff, deception, penetration. It was so pleasant to sit down with another Indian for a long morning of smokes, gossip, and business, learning all the news and driving a close bargain. Very few of his people ever came by his house, and those were mostly specimens like Yellow Singer. He did not want any one there; that was a place apart, just as here he always had the feeling of a secret knowledge he could not share, something beyond the comprehension of the men he encountered.

He listened to the gossip, jokes, and talk about women that was frank enough, seeing in it all that they had no idea of what he knew. He did not try to speak of his wife, knowing that he could never tell them about her, nor yet make a pretense of speaking as if she were just a wife, as they did. Few ever asked after her, and then in a tone of a certain constraint, though their words were formal enough. He had expected something of the sort, after what his uncle had said; she broke the rules and upset things. If they knew her, she was troublesome to them. Of course they resented the disturbance of their minds, and called it bad, with tales that grew in telling. So he sat, as it were, on the edge of their domestic discussions. When it was a matter of horses, he came to be listened to with respect. Every one agreed that he knew horses, and that he was an excellent trader; when he was speaking about a horse he was trying to sell at the moment, nothing he said was believed.

Trading was brisk and profitable. His own people were active enough in it. Hopis came down that way, and occasionally a Zuñi would pass by. A tourist company in Los Palos was having a good season; they found it convenient to tell Slim Girl that they wanted so many ponies delivered on such a day. They often got fearful catmeat, but always sound, and profitable for all with the Easterners paying two dollars a day.

His profits went back into the herd. One by one he was getting himself animals that satisfied him, that made him happy to touch and proud to ride them. When the day came that they went back to T'o Tlakai, they would bring fine blankets and much jewelry on splendid horses. He made a pair of brass-mounted saddles, and began, little by little as he earned the silver, a squaw's bridle that should be envied from the San Juan to the Little Colorado.

Those days afield ceased to be penalties. As he settled in the saddle at dawn, it was rather like reëntering the old, familiar life into which he carried the enchanted quality of the new. The trail to Natah-netinn was still cool; he loped and enjoyed himself. There would be the action of rounding up a loose pony, the pleasure of feeling a neat-footed horse under one, chance meetings, talk, and trade.

Almost best of all was to sit on a knoll, smoking and watch the animals feed. One never sees a horse so well as when he is grazing close by, intent upon the grass, oblivious of the man. Then one sees how he moves his ears, how he blows through his soft nostrils, how his casual movements are made. He moves from clump to clump, making his selections by standards of his own, never still, yet entirely free of the restlessness of a stalled horse. It is the essence of pastoral life. Cigarette smoke rises lazily in the hot air, the sun is comfortable upon one's bones, the gently moving animals make peace.

He did his thinking then, detached from his emotions, mildly introspective, reflective. He would weigh each thing and value it, go back, retrace, and balance. It was one thing to have made up his mind, another to know exactly where he was—the difference between setting out on a new trail and marking down all the landmarks of the discovered country. The horse shifted from clump to clump, making soft noises, hooves in sand, and crunching. Cigarette smoke wavered and turned with breezes too soft to feel, the movement of the heat in the air. Thoughts became pictures, changing slowly.

He had accepted Slim Girl's difference and unconventionality, but for some time still she occasionally
startled him. He wanted to understand her; he thought
he was sure of what she was, but yet admitted that
there were things about her that were beyond him. And
for some reason, he always resented the idea of her
working in the town. Not that it was a novelty for
Navajos to work for Americans, or that he had any
means of taking an attitude towards menial labour.
His people had owned slaves in the old days; a few
still survived, but he had no particular idea of the
position of a servant. Yet he wished she would not go
there. Then again, he sympathized entirely with her
idea of amassing a fortune. Perhaps it was just because
the town and its Americanism were part of an unknown
world, perhaps because when she returned from there
she seemed so tired, and once or twice he had surprised
in her eyes a puzzling look, a look of a man who has
just killed and scalped a hated enemy. But it was no
use his trying to form an opinion. He did not know
his way here; with only his people's judgments and
measures, he could decide nothing. He certainly could
not expect everything to be the same. As well expect,
when one had ridden beyond Old Age River, into the
Mormon country, to turn and still see Chiz-na Hozolchi
on the eastern horizon.

On those few occasions when she warned him that
the missionary's wife would want her to stay overnight,
he did not like to come home. He tried it once, and
found that the house without her was a long song of
emptiness. Usually he would stay with some friends
on the reservation, feeling a little patronizing towards
their family life, slightly disturbed only by the presence
of their children. Those nights he missed his drink,
finding himself with but a poor appetite for supper, and
with little desire for talk. Their food seemed coarse
to him nowadays.

Aside from all other things, going away was worth
while for the sake of coming back, well tired, to be
greeted at the house. It was so different from coming
back to T'o Tlakai. There was a thrill in riding up to
the door, particularly when he came on a newly traded,
yet finer horse. Or it was a real source of pleasure

to bring in a string for the tourist company, whooping at them as they debouched from the narrow place between the bluffs, herding and mastering them at a run, into the corral, conscious of Slim Girl leaning in the doorway, delightfully aware of her admiration. There would be news, talk, and all the magic when the sun began to set. Quite often he was first home. He would amuse himself by arranging things for supper, piling wood, drawing water. He learned to handle the can-opener. Then she would come through the opening; he would see her pace quicken as she noticed his horse in the corral, and he would sit back, smiling, to receive her smile.

II

One day he raced home before a thunderstorm that caught him just at the end, first a fine spray, then such a drenching as one might get from buckets, then the spray again, and a pale sun that had no warmth. The valley was all in shadow when he reached the house; he was wet and cold. She had not arrived yet. He built up the fire, and then, searching for coffee, came across the bottle. That was just the thing. But no, he decided, it is she who understands that, and went on looking for coffee. He found the package, empty. Well, he would try a little whiskey.

There was no fruit in the house, so he poured himself about half a mug of clear liquor. Bah! It was filthy-tasting stuff.

'Mule's water!' he said.

But even that little taste was warming. He sugared the whiskey, held his nose, and bolted it. First he felt sick to his stomach, then he began to feel better. *Ei-yei!* There was a fire in the middle of him, he was warm all over. He was walking on air. He rolled and lit a cigarette. He began to feel so well! He sang,

> 'Now with a god I walk,
> Striding the mountain-tops—'

That was the way to take it, it was fine stuff. He wished Slim Girl would come soon. He thought of many things to say to her. He would make her see how he felt about her, how beautifully he understood her. She must know what wonderful things he knew how to say, how perceptive he was. She must stop thinking about all those things she was always thinking about, and drink some of this, and sing with him. There would be such love as never had been in all the world before. To-morrow he would bring his horses and they would ride to T'o Tlakai, and if that missionary's wife said anything about it, he would shoot her and tie her scalp on his bridle. It was foolish working for her, when his jewelry and his horses were so entirely sufficient. Life in T'o Tlakai would be a dream. He could see just how beautiful it would be. A little more whiskey would be good.

It went down more easily, a second half-mug, nearer full than the last, on his empty stomach.

'T'o Tlakai and children.' He said out loud, 'I want some children.' And began to feel sorry for himself. Then he began to feel sick. He felt very sick. Everything was dark and whirling, and he was miserable. He fell upon the floor, hiding his eyes to see if things wouldn't stay still. Immediately the floor began to rise on end, higher and higher; soon he would be pitched against the wall. He opened his eyes, the floor went back to level, but the whole business span. Then he was racked. The world heaved and bucked, waters roared in his ears. Then he went out completely.

She, too, was tired when she came in, having been kept back by the storm. She looked down on him, heaved a sigh, and then smiled as a mother might whose child had done something forbidden and hurt himself just enough to learn a lesson. Very gently, she pulled him so that his head lay in the ashes. One arm fell across his spew. She put the uncorked bottle beside him, where he would smell the stuff when he came to. She nodded to herself. It was well enough, lucky to have happened just like this. It would teach him. The place did not smell very well. She took some food and a blanket, and went up to the tree on top of the bluff.

III

The corn matured and was harvested. Seedling peaches that he had set out began to lose their leaves.

First frost appeared in the night. The season of thunderstorms had passed; now was the time when one might say the names of the gods. Laughing Boy, riding herd, felt the tang in the air and touched his bow. This was good hunting weather, if one could go to the mountains. Down here there was nothing save the usual prairie dogs, coyotes, and jack rabbits. He began to feel restless.

One day he met two braves dressed in all their best and fanciest, one on a roan and one on a pinto. His own horse, freshly caught, was prancing as he rode up to them; theirs were lively.

'*Ahalani!*'

'*Ahalani,* Grandfather!'

'Where are you going?'

'To dance at Chilbito. And you, say?'

'Just riding around. I have horses here.'

'You have a good horse.'

'He is pretty good. I got him from a Hopi. Let us race.'

'Good. How much will you bet?'

'Five dollars.

'That is too much for us; bet three.'

'Good. To that tree there?'

'All right.'

Hé! His horse did well. Too bad he didn't have the bay. '*E-é-é-ya!* Come on now, my horse, come on, Grandfather!' Three horses tearing neck and neck, three men bent over their manes, urging. The pinto was nosing ahead. Laughing Boy pressed in his heels, his belly drew tight with the thrill of motion.

They hurtled past the tree, the pinto slightly ahead, and drew rein, laughing.

'You win, Grandfather.'

The man received his money.

'I am sorry I did not have my bay horse here. He is much faster than this one.'

'Bring your bay horse to the dance. There may be some racing, I think.'

'What dance is it?'

'A Night Chant. Wind Singer is leading it.'

'I shall think about coming.'

'It is only a five-day dance. It is for Twice Brave;

he has not much money, they say. You had better come soon.'

'What made him sick?'

'He looked at his mother-in-law; he spoke to her, they say.'

'Ei-yei! How did that happen?'

'They lived near each other. When his wife was away, she got his food for him, they say. He came too soon and saw her. She covered her face, but he spoke to her, they say.'

'He spoke to her! He is crazy, I think.'

'Perhaps he is; he does strange things. When the missionary at Tsé Tlchi used to serve beans, a lot of us went to hear him. He held a sing every seven days, and afterwards there were beans, but there was no dancing. We followed the Jesus Road until he stopped giving us beans. Then Twice Brave went back and stole a lot of red *t'oghlepai* that he had, it was something to do with his religion. It was good. But when he had drunk a lot of it, he went and made his horse drink it. He put the bottle down its mouth and made it take it, the way he had seen an American do. He made his horse crazy, just like a man. I saw it. It couldn't walk straight. And now he has spoken to his mother-in-law, they say. So he has a bad toothache. You should come to the dance.'

'Ei! I should like to see that man. I shall come if I can.'

He was glad that the season of the great dances was returning. As he rode home, he thought that it would be good to see the gods once more, perhaps to know the holy fear and exaltation when one swallowed the sacred arrows inside the Dark Circle of Branches. He loved the gatherings of people, the huge fires, and the holy things. There was religious experience and high thought, and then there was sociability on a large scale. Sometimes there were horse-races or a chicken-pull or gambling.

He had not thought about these things for so long, or at least he had thought of them distantly, himself apart. As a blanket and its design before dawn is seen, but has no colours, then with clear light grows vivid in red and green and yellow, so the feeling of his tribe swept over him. It was exhilarating.

IV

He spoke about it to her after supper. 'There is to be a Night Chant over at Chilbito, by Tseye Buckho. There may be racing.'

'How long will the song last?' There was no reason in the world why they should not go. She was searching in her mind, and found only that she dreaded it.

'Only five nights. It is for Twice Brave; he is not very rich, they say.'

'We do not want to go, I think. Let us wait for a complete one.'

She understood herself as she spoke; she was jealous of his people, of something they had in common which she could not share.

He looked at her inquiringly, catching a tone of earnestness in her voice. She had no reasons, yet very much did not want to go. He saw that it mattered to her.

'Perhaps you are right. We shall wait.'

'I think that is better'

Both understood.

It was puzzling, though. He wondered about it as they sat there. He wanted to understand her. He told himself: 'If she wants me to know, she will tell me. I do not think she knows herself. I have made up my mind, there is no use hesitating on the trail. I make her my life, let her be my life. I do not know why she does this thing, but I know what I think of her. If I knew just what was in her mind, it would be worth thinking about, it would tell me something about her. Now there is so much of her I do not understand. I know what I want, that is enough.'

He watched her in the firelight, her slender lines, her oval face of sleeping fires. The trail of beauty lay within this house; not all the songs and horses in the world were worth this minute.

CHAPTER ELEVEN

I

THE life apart enclosed him again. If some encounter with Indians bound for a dance, some reminiscent incident, brought on a momentary restlessness, he did not have to deal with it. It simply expressed itself in the smug feeling that what he had was so vastly superior to anything in their philosophy. He was a little sorry for those people. When he felt like that, he would stir his pony to a lope, with his head high, uplifted, thinking of Slim Girl, of some little thing to say or do for her. He was a young man very much in love, a young man with his mind made up to love.

At the beginning of the month of Little Snow, he surprised her by bringing an Indian home with him. She was disturbed and uneasy as she prepared the extra food. There was no reason to be bothered; just because something had never happened before did not make it a bad sign. Underneath all her self-confidence was a feeling which she refused to recognize, that this life of theirs hung by threads. Really, in her heart of hearts, she was surprised that everything ran so smoothly. Little things upset her.

Long-haired and hatless, the man's pure Navajo costume, the heavy look of his jewelry, indicated the Northern country. Laughing Boy called him cousin, and questioned him about people and things at T'o Tlakai and all the Gyende district. The eager voice and the old, familiar names, the home things: she was afraid of all those people, those words. Life was lonely here. Perhaps if she were to keep him, she would have to give up and move back among his own kind. She observed to herself that this man, who was to bind her to The People, seemed to be driving her yet farther apart from them.

When they were alone for a minute, he said, 'Why did you not give me my drink? Why did you not offer him one?'

'That drink is medicine that I know. You must leave it to me. There are things that must not be done about it, just like prayer-sticks and sacred cigarettes.' As she spoke, she prepared a stiff dose. 'That man must not have it or know about it. You must not speak of it unless I say you may.'

'Good, then, I hear you.' He drained it off. He had missed it.

'I was afraid you would speak of it before him.'

'I thought about it. You had some reason, I thought. So I waited.'

She nodded.

'He is my uncle's son; not Wounded Face at Tsé Lani, another one from T'o Tlakai. His sister is sick. They are going to hold a full Night Chant, ten nights. They want us to come, he says. Mountain Singer wants me to dance in it; it is a song that I know well. I have been in it before when he led.'

His voice told her, 'This time I want to go. Now you must do something for me.' She saw that it would be a mistake to oppose him.

'Let us go, then; I think it will be a good thing. I shall be glad to see your country and your people, and a big dance like that is always good to go to.' There was under-pleading in her voice, but he knew that this was a gift to him. 'When is the dance to be?'

'At the full of Little Snow Moon.'

It was obvious that he looked forward eagerly to the visit. This was to be her test that was coming, one more test, and she felt there were enough already. She excelled herself in tenderness and charm, and strengthened his drinks. His response to her was evidence of a steadily burning fire that would momentarily lull her doubts. In every act and word and look he seemed to testify his steadfastness, but still she was uneasy.

On the night before the start for T'o Tlakai, they

sat late by the fire. He spoke eagerly of his own country, while she answered little. The colourful cliffs and cañons, the warm rock, the blue masses of distant mountains—

'When it gets all hot there in the valley, when it is sunlight in the little crevices, and everything you look at seems to jump out at you, you look over towards the east. Just above the rim of the cliffs you see Chiz-na Hozolchi Mountain. It is far away, it is blue and soft. Even when the sky is blue as turquoise and hard as a knife-blade, it is soft, and more blue. You will like that country.'

Is he trying to persuade me to stay there? Perhaps we shall have to, in the end. I shall need all my strength.

'It will be fine when we ride in together. We shall have two good ponies. They will envy our jewelry. They will envy my saddle-blanket that you made me.'

And they will know about me, and his own people will talk to him.

'They are good people. You will like them.'

They are my enemies, more than if they were Utes.

When he fell silent, he would touch her arm with his finger-tips. Then he would speak again, staring into the fire as a man will when he is seeing something, but always turning to look at her, almost shyly.

She relaxed, relieved of her fear. I am a fool. I am a crazy damned fool. I am the centre of all that he is thinking. He is all tied up in me. He cares for this and that, but I am the door through which it all comes. Listen to the way he is talking, see how he looks. We can go to a thousand dances and he will still be mine. Not all The People in the world can take him away. If he is ever lost to me, it will be I who have lost him.

She moved over and leant against him, her head on his shoulder. 'I think your country will be very beautiful. I shall be glad to see it. Your people will not like me, I think, but I do not care, if we are together.'

II

Slim Girl's idea of travel on horseback was that

one should ride during the cooler part of the morning, rest out the noon downpour of light and heat in a shady place, and use the last of the day to find the nearest friendly hogahn. There could be none of that now, she knew. Her man was a Navajo and a horseman, when he settled in the saddle, as the sides of his calves touched his pony's barrel, and he felt the one current run through them, there was always that little look of uplift. Probably half of the waking hours of his life had been spent on a horse's back, but not the longest day could destroy in him a certain pleasure in even the workaday jog or mechanical, mile-eating lope of a good pony.

She thought of this, as they skirted Los Palos in the dawn, and sighed, foreseeing heat and fatigue, stiffness and soreness in unromantic places, all to be concealed from this man of hers. He did not even know that it was necessary for one to be toughened to the saddle; he thought people were born that way, if he thought about it at all. She wondered, doubting, if any of the exaltation of their first ride to Los Palos would carry her through this.

It was not so bad as she had feared. At this late time of year it was hardly hot even at midday. Her weaving and occasional hours in the cornfield had hardened her somewhat. The high-cantled Navajo saddle he had made for her, with its seat of slung leather over which a dyed goatskin was thrown, was more comfortable than one would have thought possible. The miles stretched out before them, shrank, and were overpassed. She was tired in the late afternoon, thirsty from dust, silent. She watched this man who rode before her, so easy in his saddle, so at home, going back to his own country.

She no longer had her own, different background. She was afraid because of him. It was no longer she who was strong, leading, marking the places for him to set down his feet. Now it was she who must fumble, uncertain, and he who must hold her up. What hobbles would she have on him now? It was all right, that he felt all for her, that she was the centre of things, but how could she be sure when his own people and his own things spoke to him? There was nothing to do but wait and be watchful, and meantime a little mouse was gnawing at her heart.

They spent the night at a friendly hogahn. There, too, he was at home and she astray. She saw his natural sociability expand in the evening gossip, and she learned with surprise that he had an established place among these people, who looked at her faintly askance. He was already known, and his opinions on horses were listened to with respect.

She had been drawn to him first just because of these things. She wanted him as a link between herself and just such as these people. But more, terribly more now, she needed him, himself completely hers with no fragment left out, and so they had become her enemies.

Yet there was plenty with which to comfort herself. Their opinion of her changed visibly when they learned that it was she who had woven Laughing Boy's saddle-blanket. The red background, with the black and white interlocked fret of the heat lightning, was a gay and handsome thing. The women examined it, felt its weave, and spoke highly of it. There was an evident, kind-hearted relief at this proof that she was regular.

More important was the subtle difference, the special quality of her husband's attitude towards her when compared with their host and his wife. In that house was the usual peace and understanding of an Indian's home, but there was none of that faint reverence and intimate desire that she felt when Laughing Boy spoke to her. She knew she should be proud and happy, but sleep was long in coming as they lay in their blankets about the dying fire.

The second day was like the first, save that, instead of growing stiff and sore, she grew stiffer and sorer. Her fears rode with her behind the saddle; she wondered after her old, arrogant sureness.

They made camp for themselves, having come to a section where no one lived. She was unhappy in mind and body, not overjoyed at their roofless stopping place and the prospect of a cold night, nor pleased with bread and coffee and a little dried meat. After supper they sat in silence, smoking and looking into the coals. She thought that silence was inimical.

At last he said; 'I shall set a trap back there by those rocks; we should have a prairie-dog for breakfast.

They are good. I know you do not care for this food we just had. You are used to better.'

'I do not mind. You must not think about me.'

'I wish you had brought some of that whiskey. Since you have taught me that, everything is flat without it. There is no salt in things. I missed it last night, and I do now.'

'I brought some. I did not know you wanted it. Here is about enough for two drinks. You will have to take it just plain.'

'That is all right. Give me some, then.'

He drank his dose eagerly.

'There will be none of that at T'o Tlakai,' she told him.

'That is all right. It does not belong there; it is part of the new world you have made for me. I do not think I could go back to just living, like these other people.'

She thought to herself, that is well enough, while we are alone. You will lose the need for the drink in the time we are there, perhaps you will forget about it.

None the less she felt better, and noticed that the night was beautiful with stars. After all, camping thus was part of her people's heritage. She was doing a Navajo thing. Her blanket sufficed to keep her warm; she fell asleep as soon as she closed her eyes.

As they went farther north, at first the desert rather appalled her. She was accustomed to the southeastern part of the Navajo country, grey bluffs, and grey rolling plateaus and harshly monotonous, distant mountains. Since she had known fertile California and the bustle and comfort of the places where ciilized man gathers together to domesticate the scenery, she had never been able to feel any deep liking for the empty desert and the hostile fury of its silence. Now they were come among warm, golden cliffs, painted with red and purplish brown and luminous shadows, a broken country that changed with the changing sun, narrow cañons, great mesas, yellow sands, and distant, blue mountains.

They rode along a defile, scarcely a hundred yards wide, whose walls, twice as high, looked as though they had just drawn apart, and might decide to close again. Scrub oak, in the bottom, clustered along a running stream. The place was full of shadow. Looking up, one saw magnificent, dark firs growing along the ledges and hanging valleys. Up there, the ruddy rock, touched by the sunlight, became dull orange and buff, with flecks of gold, and a golden line where it met a flawless sky. Their horses' feet made a tiny, soft noise in the sand. Nested on one ledge was a village of the long-vanished Old People, square little stone houses high up, with black spots of doorways that watched the cañon. Laughing Boy pointed to the ruin.

'Yota Kien,' he said. 'Some of the Divine Ones live there, they say. The two brothers came here when they were looking for Talking God, they say.'

They stopped to rest and water the horses. She looked about her, feeling the quiet, absorbing the place. She had a sense of rest and of growth. She had not known that one could feel intimate about anything so grand.

He brought her to a high place late one afternoon, a spur of Dzhil Clizhini. It had been a fatiguing, scrambling climb, with one piece to be done on foot, alleviated by the increasing growth of jack pine and spruce. At length they trotted along a level, following a winding path under firs. There was a short stretch of broken ground, grey, knobbed rock, oaks whose branches one had to duck, a tumbling little gorge at the left, with the smell of water. They were shut in by trees.

He drew rein, motioning to her to come up beside him. She did so, crowding past the twigs that hemmed in the path. Right before their horses' feet the cliff fell away, some fourteen hundred feet, and there, under their hands, lay all the North Country. It was red in the late sunlight, fierce, narrow cañons with ribbons of shadow, broad valleys and lesser hills streaked with purple opaque shadows like deep holes in the world, cast by the upthrust mesas. The great, black volcanic core of Agathla was a sombre monstrosity in the midst of colour. Away and away it stretched, jumbled, vast, the crazy shapes of the Monuments, the clay hills of Utah, and far beyond everything, floating blue mountain shapes softer than the skies. She drew back in the saddle.

'When any one comes here, even if he has been here many times, it hits him in the face. Wait and look, by and by you grow until you can take all this inside of you. Then nothing can make you angry or disturb you.'

They sat in silence, looking, absorbing. He dismounted, added one to a cairn of stones, and squatted, gazing out. There was something about it that made Slim Girl choke. It made her want to cry.

The trail led down over the face of the cliff in an alarming manner, a test for sure-footed ponies. Below, it was all thick shadow. Their animals, stepping delicately, were taking them down from sunlight into late evening.

You, too, have your magic, your strong medicine, Laughing Boy, and I think it is greater than mine. This is what I want you for. Some day we shall put our two magics together; some day you will bring me here, to have this always. You will bring me, if it does not take you from me first.

III

At length they were reaching T'o Tlakai, riding down a slope of bald rock into a valley about three miles square, surrounded by moderately high cliffs. Here and there, at their feet, were clumps of scrub oak, peach trees, and the marks of summer cornfields, where water seeped out under the rocks. Along the north cliff was a long ledge, with the rock above it rising in a concave shell of light reflected under shadow. Along the ledge stretched an imposing ruin of the Old People, at one end of which, where there must be a spring, a strip of grass showed very green. Down the middle of the valley spindly cottonwoods marked the course of the wash. The rest was dull and colourless— sand hills, sand, rocks, sagebrush, greasewood, some sheep. Nearly in the centre were five hogahns, two square ones of leaves, deserted now that winter was at hand, and three dome-shaped mud ones. The framework of the medicine-lodge for the dance had already been set up. There were a good many horses tethered around the settlement.

It did not look like much, but she found it threatening, inimical. She wanted some sign; it would have been a relief if people had come buzzing out as they appeared over the brow of the rock, if there had been shouts of anger, anything. The houses were more than a mile away still. Would they be clever people or stupid, hostile, friendly, or resigned? Were they able opponents or could she conquer them? The quiet houses fascinated her. Just she against all those, against everything here, these rocks, these underfed trees, those far-off mountains, the little bushes. She had fought against worse, but this meant so much. The horses seemed barely to crawl.

Ahead of her, Laughing Boy was singing a hymn, half aloud:

> 'Dawn Boy Hill rises,
> Jewels Hill rises,
> White Corn Hill rises . . .
> Those people their fields, my fields, now
> they rise all beautiful before me!'

CHAPTER TWELVE

I

DURING the greetings, Laughing Boy took stock. With entire confidence in his wife's ability to win over these people, he carried himself as though he had no faintest idea that there might be strained relations between them, but in his mind he was calling the roll of his family. Wounded Face, sitting apart in his blanket like a sleepy eagle, was against him. Spotted Horse, the younger uncle, was waiting; meantime he intended to be cordial. Spotted Horse would follow somebody's lead, whoever spoke most commandingly; afterwards, if the issue were unpleasant, he would mildly deplore it. His mother was against him, but she too waited, not declaring herself, not closing her judgment yet. His sisters took no position, but welcomed the stranger and did their best to make her at home because she was his wife. Bow's Son, his brother, and Bay Horse, his brother-in-law, both evidently thought he had made a fool of himself, and felt hostile towards her. Bay Horse could be discounted; he did not belong to the clan, and the taboo which forbids a man's looking upon his mother-in-law kept him away from the family circle most of the time.

Out of the corner of his eye, without seeming to pay attention, he watched Slim Girl with relish as she said and did exactly the right things, giving an excellent impersonation of just any attractive woman.

Now Jesting Squaw's Son dismounted before the hogahn and stood beside him, looking anxious and hesitant. It was plain to see that he was concerned only lest there should be some estrangement between them, lest an alien life might have made a gulf. Friendship stood firm and true. So they embraced and wrestled and spoke loudly to each other.

He faced his father last, and most anxiously. Two Bows had held back from the others; his was an awkward position in this matter. Long days of teaching the jeweller's craft, hunts together, lessons in the trail and the bow, work shared, had brought them very near to each other. They were father and son, and they were close friends. Laughing Boy admired and emulated the old warrior, and he could confide in him. Two Bows saw some of himself bearing fruit anew in the young brave. And yet, in a matter like this, his rights were only those of courtesy—to Laughing Boy's own clansmen, to his mother and her brothers, was the decision. He could only watch for the time when his purely personal influence might turn the scales. Now, he said nothing. His son could feel fondness and sympathy there, but whether approval went with it he could not tell.

Laughing Boy had been half-afraid lest, like Friend of the Eagles, or Reared in a Mountain, he would find that his own people seemed dirty and smelled badly when he returned to them. Secretly, even a little shamefacedly, he considered the life that he was living perhaps not so far removed from that of ordinary Earth People as the Eagles' home in the sky, or the mother-of-pearl and turquoise dwellings of the Divine Ones, but still something apart, like the magic country at the end of Old Age River. He had waited somewhat anxiously for his first impression, and found that his home was delightfully as he had imagined it. Everything was the same; it seemed a miracle. That which had been intimate and dear was so still, only now nothing was taken for granted, but every commonest detail leapt to him with new vividness.

There were constant little surges of delight in his heart over trivial, minor things—a shadow across a cliff, the bend of a cottonwood, the sheep coming in at evening, their silly, solemn faces all about the hogahn—why should they have changed? A man does not realize that he has changed himself, or only partially recognizes it, thinking that the world about him is different; a familiar dish has become no longer enjoyable, a fundamental aphorism no longer true; it is a surprise, then, when his eyes and ears report unchanged, familiar impressions. So the wonderful sameness of things, the unfailing way in which expectation was fulfilled, were proofs of something beautiful in the order of the world. It was glorious to pick up the threads of talk where he had dropped them, discussing the old, well-worn subjects casually and in detail, as though they were still inlaid in his life, with just a little seasoning of the attitude of one who has been farther and seen more.

One could see that his family had expected some outlandishness. Now they were puzzled; some disappointed, and some pleased to see how normal and Navajo were Laughing Boy and his wife. Her blankets spoke for them with many tongues, and the solid evidences of their prosperity, all Navajo, nothing bizarre or American, but good honest silver, turquoise, coral—'hard goods'—and handsome Indian ponies.

He watched Slim Girl, seeing the shutters closed behind her eyes, correct, sure, in hand, doing just the perfect thing. He was swept by constantly recurring waves of pleasure in her, and felt, as he sometimes did, a faint fear of that detached self-command. Slowly they were being forced to accept her as really belonging to the People. It pleased his dramatic instinct, as well as the strong sense of privacy he had concerning their relationship, to play up, being very normal, and letting no look or gesture suggest that they two came from a land of enchantment.

Knowing her well, he could see that she was at high tension, and secretly watchful. He had no idea that that strain, that painful vigilance, was above all for himself.

When he was alone with his father, he showed him the silver-mounted bridle and some of his other jewelry. Two Bows turned over the harness, feeling the surface with his finger-tips.

'I have nothing more to teach you—that is well done.' He tapped the cheek-strap. 'I should not have thought of using that design that way.'

From Two Bows, such praise made it hard to keep a quiet, modest face.

Jesting Squaw's Son came back in the late afternoon. They drifted off together, with arms over each other's shoulders, until they came to rest under the scrub oaks behind the peach trees. They discussed this and that, vaguely, trailing off into silence, playing with twigs and pebbles, running their fingers through the sand, occupying their hands. At length Laughing Boy looked at his friend and spoke:

'I do not talk to those people. Some of them have their minds made up, some of them will not understand. I do not think you will know what I am talking about, but you understand me. I want you to know.

'I have been down Old Age River in the log, with sheet-lightning and rainbows and soft rain, and the gods on either side to guide me. The Eagles have put lightning snakes and sunbeams and rainbows under me; they have carried me through the hole in the sky.

I have been through the little crack in the rocks with Red God and seen the homes of the Butterflies and the Mountain Sheep and the Divine Ones. I have heard the Four Singers on the Four Mountains. I mean that woman.

'It sounds like insane talk. It is not. It is not just because I am in love. It is not what I feel when I am near her, what happens to my blood when she touches me. I know about that. I have thought about that. It is what goes on there. It is all sorts of things, but you would have to live there to see it.

'I know the kind of thing my uncle says. It is not true. We are not acting out here, we are pretending. We have masks on, so they will not see our real faces. You have seen her blankets and my hard goods. Those are true. Those are just part of it.'

Jesting Squaw's Son answered, 'I have seen the blankets and the hard goods; they sing. I am happy about you.'

He felt better after that, he cared that his friend should know, and, in contradistinction to the others, telling him did not lessen the rare quality of the thing described. He returned to the hogahns feeling better able to act his part.

He found the evening meal most enjoyable as he watched the good ways and mannerisms of his family. Among them he could make out a growing perplexity. What had that old man told them to expect? A word slipped from his brother to his younger uncle gave him the cue, filling his heart with glee. When he got a chance he whispered to Slim Girl,

'What my uncle said—they expected you to have no manners. They were waiting for you to act like an American, and give them something to talk about.'

He lolled back on the sheepskins, laughing inside himself. A smile shadowed the corners of his wife's mouth.

III

Slim Girl watched the ceremony with interest, feeling in a pronounced fashion the mixed emotion she had towards so much that was going on about her. It might be a weapon to destroy her, for the very reason that

106

it was a summation and a visible expression of many things in her people's life that mattered to her. She had a sneaking suspicion that the family had gone to the expense of a full Night Chant largely because of the effect they thought it might have on the erring member.

It was sometimes absurd and sometimes quite beautiful. The masked dancers were grotesque, but there were moments by firelight when their shapeless heads and painted bodies, their rhythmic, intent movements, became grand and awe-inspiring. The long and repetitious prayers were often monotonous, chanted to dull, heavy music, but in the worst of them there were flashes of poetic feeling. Her American education had dulled her sensibility to the quick, compact imagery of a single statement, leaving to the hearer, the evocation of the picture intended that forms the basis of Navajo poetry. Still, she caught it sometimes,

'By red rocks the green corn grows,
    Beautifully it grows . . .'

She saw it, and the terse implication that takes for granted all that the Indians feel about corn, contenting itself with merely calling forth that feeling.

She tried to think that these things were native and close to her, but found that she could only observe them objectively. She was foreign now. She could sympathize with their spirit, but not enter into it. A door had been closed to her, and at times, even standing here among the other spectators, in the heart of the Navajo country, she was swept again by a hopeless nostalgia for the country and the people, forever lost, of her dim childhood.

When she had been a very little girl, she had trembled with terror and awe at the sight of the very gods coming into the circle of people. Out in the darkness one heard their distant call, repeated as they came nearer, until with the fourth cry they entered the firelight. They danced and sang there, majestic and strange; then they vanished again to return to their homes in the sacred places. Now they were just Indians whom she knew, dressed up in a rather silly way. Like many unreligious people, she kept slipping into the idea that these worshippers were pretending to be taken in by the patently absurd. Most of the adult spectators had been through the Night Chant initiation; all of them knew that the gods were no more than men in masks; how could they be so reverent? What was her devout husband's ecstasy, or his devoutness, when he himself put on the painted rawhide bag trimmed with spruce and feathers, pretending to be Talking God?

She remembered the sacrament at school when she had been Christian. She had known that the wine came from the vineyard of an Italian who was a Catholic—something vaguely wicked—and that the bread was just bread. She knew the minister for a nice man whose wife rather bullied him. Yet she had believed that Christ's blood appeared in the wine, or something like that, and had been uplifted when she partook of it.

A Klamath girl had cried bitterly before her first communion. It came out that she feared that eating Christ would make her conceive. In a legend of her own people, Raven had made a woman conceive that way. The minister had been very patient with her, and afterwards the other girls had made fun of her.

The casual way in which the minister handled the jug of wine when it came used to shock her, yet when he raised the chalice, his face would be inspired. He knew it was just the Italian's wine and himself, but he had not been pretending.

These Navajos were just like that. She couldn't make it seem reasonable to herself, but she understood it. And what effect would it have on Laughing Boy?

During the day she occupied herself with the women's work of preparing the semi-sacramental ceremonial foods. She knew very little, indeed, about the ancient ways of cooking, but her sisters-in-law taught her. They were prepared to like her. Her bad reputation had reached them only vaguely, and already they were discrediting it, so that she became to them some one somehow belonging to a larger world, said to be dangerous, hence superior. Now they found her ignorant in this matter, humble, and anxious to learn. She was normal, then, what their slight experience had taught them to expect of returned school-girls, who were always to be pitied. They were delighted to make her their protégée and have the feeling of taking this woman of the world under their wing. Her warm response was not all acting, either; it was not often that women of any race were friendly to her without reservations.

Their mother, she saw, was merely conscientiously fulfilling the ceremonial requirement that every one should feel kind towards every one else during the days of the dance. That atmosphere of *'hozoji'* pervaded the whole camp with a sweetness that was saved from being laughable by the deep devotion behind it. The time of trial was not yet. Slim Girl had some cause to be happy, and so fell in with the general frame of mind, finding a certain reality of meaning in the eternally repeated 'trail of beauty,' 'walking in beauty,' of the ceremony.

In a sentimental way she played at believing her people's religion, and indeed began to find some truth in its basic doctrine, but when she attempted to extend acceptance to the forms which she observed, her sense of the grotesque made it a farce. Meantime she was conquering these people; some were her friends already; her enemies were checked and nonplussed. The opening skirmishes, at least, were hers. She was moving ever more in the stream of Navajo life. She did have cause to be happy. The religion might remain meaningless to her, and probably always would, but the underlying concept of the active force of *'hozoji'* became real.

IV

The men who took part in the dance kept pretty well by themselves. For several days she did not speak to her husband. It was during the fifth afternoon that, seeing him go over where the sun warmed a rock to snatch some sleep, she followed and sat down beside him. She dreamed, watching his face. She loved him so much. There was that love, enough in itself, and then there was so much more. As she had hoped, after all, he was the means of returning to the good things of the Navajo, the good things of life. She could not lose him. What would happen when the dance was over, when it was time to leave, when old Wounded Face showed his hand? She was dependent on this man, her husband; she could not lose him.

She smoked and waited. At length he woke. She reached out and drew her fingers across the back of his hand.

'You must not do that.'

'Why not?'

'I am thinking about the Holy Things. I have to concern my mind only with them. You should not have come here.'

'Is it bad to think about me? Are your thoughts of me not—*hozoji*?' She smiled.

He remained grave. 'They are *hozoji,* but they are not all of it. When I think about the whole, I am thinking about you, too. I give thanks for you. But I must not just think about you and forget all the rest. Now, go away.'

'I see.'

She went softly. Two voices spoke within her; one, that this was the beginning of destruction; the other, that this meant nothing; indeed, that it was a good sign that her presence could disturb him so. Overriding both opinions was a feeling that, unless she was the whole for him, she could not be sure of holding him, and her imperiousness rebelled at being ever subordinate.

And still the ceremony was only half over. What would the remainder bring? She watched the changing rites. The ninth night passed, and the tenth day. She marvelled at the men's endurance; they had periods of rest, but there were night vigils, and for Mountain Singer, endless preparatory prayers. He did not seem tired; rather one would say that he drew rest and strength from his songs. She was sorry for the sick girl, a passive bundle of blankets inside the medicine hogahn, sadly in need of quiet and fresh air.

During that last day visitors began to arrive, until two or three hundred were camped in the valley. There was a slaughtering of sheep and wholesale boiling of coffee and tea. Slim Girl was kept gratefully busy helping in the preparations. The tenth night, with the rite of the Grandfather of the Gods, was the climax.

It was a fine spectacle, the many dancing figures in the firelight, their strange masks and the dull earth-colours, blue, red, white, yellow, black—a broad white zigzag across a black chest, a red figure on blue, outlined with white, standing out in the half-light of the fire. The dancers were never more intent, the chanting more ecstatic. There was real dramatic quality in the entrance of the Grandfather. She was interested, excited. These were her people, putting themselves in touch with eternal forces by means of voice, strength, rhythm, colour, design—everything they had to use. They were creating something strong and barbaric and suitable, and still beautiful.

'In beauty it is finished,
In beauty it is finished,
In beauty it is finished,
In beauty it is finished!'

V

The next day was one of let-down and much sleeping. By dusk, most of the visitors had ridden away. After supper, Laughing Boy's mother and uncles went over to one of the deserted summer hogahns. He finished his cigarette and followed. Wounded Face returned and spoke to Two Bows, who went back with him. Mountain Singer rode in, dismounted, and joined them.

So she was not to be allowed to fight for herself. None of the others at the fire paid any attention; not even casting an extra glance towards Slim Girl. She remembered vaguely that, when a marriage-contract was under discussion, it was the correct thing for the girl concerned to go well away from the house. She supposed that some such etiquette could be invoked to cover this occasion. It would have to do. She slipped out into the darkness, watching to see if her going caused any commentary of exchanged looks. Then she went swiftly away from the hogahns, past the corral, where she deliberately startled a herd-dog into barking.

She circled behind to come up on the summer hogahn, carefully now, thinking of the silent feet and quick ears of her people, feeling herself clumsy, her limbs managed by indirect control. She crouched in the shadow of the back wall, clutching her blanket about her for warmth, praying that her teeth would not chatter. She was clearly conscious of the beauty of the night, its stars and sharp cold, the smell of sage and sand, the faint rustle of leaves on the hogahn.

They were lighting a fire. When it was burning well, they gathered close to it, so that peering between the leaves and branches she saw them as dim, significant masses with their faces faintly shown, identifying them. Mountain Singer was in the place of honour, with his back to her; on his left sat Walked Around, Laughing Boy's mother; on his right was Spotted Horse. Wounded Face was next to him, facing Laughing Boy, and Two Bows sat a little bit back, near the door. She summed them up to herself, wishing she could be present to use her skill and have her share in the approaching conflict. It was not fair. She wished she could see Mountain Singer's face; that old man's influence would be emphasized, now that he was just through conducting the chant, and her husband with serving him as acolyte. He was the leader of the Tahtchini Clan in this section; his importance was shown by his seat of honour in this conclave of people to whom he was only distantly related. Spotted Horse did not amount to much. Walked Around hated her, personally and with fear. Wounded Face was set against her for more general, but weighty reasons. As for Two Bows, she could not tell. He had a quality of understanding which might make him her friend or her most dangerous enemy. In any case, he was here only as a privileged outsider.

The fire began to make warmth, and tobacco was passed round. Nobody spoke for several minutes. Then Mountain Singer said:

'We are thinking about my younger brother here; we are thinking about what he should do. We have come here to talk it over with him.'

They went on smoking. They were sombre bundles of shadow, in their blankets, with faces of people faintly seen. Wounded Face spat out a grain of tobacco. 'My nephew, we do not think it is good, this thing you are doing. We have talked about it a long time among ourselves. We know about that woman, that she—'

Laughing Boy raised his head. 'You have said those things once, uncle, and I have heard them. Do not say them again, those things. If you do, there will not be any talk. Tell yourself that I have heard them,

112

and know what I think of them. They were said in Killed a Navajo's hogahn. I heard them there. Now go on from that.'

They talked, watching the end of their cigarettes, or with the right hand rubbing over the fingers of the left, as though to bring the words out, or touching each finger-tip in turn, with their eyes upon their hands, so that the even voices seemed utterly detached, the persons mere media for uttering thoughts formed at the back of nowhere.

'Perhaps you are mistaken, I think, but I do as you say. You are making unhappiness for yourself, you are making ugliness. You are of The People, the good life for you is theirs. It is all very well now while your eyes and your ears and your nose are stopped up with love, but one day you will look around and see only things that do not fit you, alkali-water to drink. You will want your own things, and you will not be able to fit them, either, I think.

'It is all very well that you deceive the younger people with your clothes and hard goods and manners, but we can see that all the time you are apart. And you are just a light from her fire, just something she has made. She has acted and spoken well here, that one. She speaks above and below and before and behind, but she does not speak straight out forward, I think.'

'We live like other People.'

'Even your beginning was like Americans. You talked about it with each other, you two arranged it face to face. You had no shame. She caused that. Have you been married?'

'Yes.'

'Who sang?'

'Yellow Singer.'

'Did you look at him? No, I think. You looked at him with your eyes, so as not to fall over him when you walked past; did your mind see him? No, I think. If you think now about him, you will see him, perhaps. You will see what is left of a man when he leaves our way, when he walks in moccasins on the Americans' road. You have seen other People who live down there. Some of them are rich, but their hearts are empty. You have seen them without happiness or beauty in their

113

hearts, because they have lost the Trail of Beauty. Now they have nothing to put in their hearts except whiskey.'

Slim Girl winced.

'Those people cannot dance in a chant and do any good. You would not want Yellow Singer to hold a chant over you, it would not bring you *hozoji*.

'You say live like The People. Why do you live apart, then? Does she not like to be with The People, that woman?

'I have spoken.'

Laughing Boy made a gesture of brushing aside. His uncle threw his cigarette butt into the fire with an angry motion.

Walked Around leaned forward. 'What my brother says is good, but it is not all, what he has said. I have watched you, how you go about. This valley T'o Tlakai speaks to you with tongues, I think. When you look over to Chiz-na Hozolchi you hear singing, I think. You hasten to speak with your own people, you like to use your tongue for old names. You care more to talk about our sheep and our waterholes—your waterholes—than we do. You belong with us, and we want you. We want good for you. When you are gone, we know that you are away. That woman keeps you from us. Why does she do it? If she means good towards you and we mean good towards you, why should she be afraid of us? Perhaps because she wants to make you into something else, she does it. Perhaps because if you were among us you would see straight.

'She has no parents, no uncles, that she should build her hogahn near them. There are plenty of the Bitahni Clan here; let her come here. Come and live among us, your own people. Perhaps then, if she is not bad, we shall see that we are wrong, we shall learn to love her, my child.'

Clever, clever, you bitch!

Laughing Boy moved his hand again.

Wounded Face took up the word. 'You are young, you do not like to listen.'

His voice was level, but he was angry; there was tension in the hut. That was good; if they showed anger they would lose him forever.

114

'You do not intend to hear what we say.'

Mountain Singer interrupted him. 'His father taught him to hunt, to dance, and to work silver. His father knows him best of us all, I think. Grandfather, what is in your mind?'

This was more important than anything heretofore.

Two Bows spoke slowly. 'We have all seen his silver, her blankets. We have seen him dance. We know, therefore, how he is now. We know that, now, all is well with him.

'A man makes a design well because he feels it. When he makes some one else's design, you can tell. If he is to make some one else's design, he must feel it in himself first. You cannot point a pistol at a man and say, "Make heat-lightning and clouds with tracks-meeting under them, and make it beautiful."

'My son is thinking about a design for his life. Let him tell us, and if it is not good, perhaps we can show him.'

'You have spoken well, Grandfather.'

'Yes, you have spoken well.' It was Spotted Horse's only contribution.

They all shifted slightly, watching Laughing Boy. He spoke without hesitation, but selecting his words precisely.

'I had not spoken, because I thought all your minds were made up. Now I shall tell you. I heard what my uncle told me that time; I saw Yellow Singer and those others down there. I have thought about all those things. I have not just run in like a crazy horse. Everything has been new, and I have watched and thought.

'I have been with that woman many moons now. I tell you that I know that those bad things are not true. Hear me.

'It is true that our life is different, but we are not following the American trail. Do not think it, that thing. She is different. She does everything as we do, more than most school-girls; but she is different. You have seen our silver, our blankets; if you come to us you will see how everything is like that. It is beautiful. It is the Trail of Beauty. You will just have to believe me, it is something I never imagined, we have nothing here to compare with it, that life. We do only good things. Everything good that I have ever known, all

115

at once, could not make me as happy as she and her way do.

'Look at me. I am older than when I left here, I know what I say. My mind is made up. I do not want you to be angry with me; I do not want you to be unhappy about me; I do not want you to tell me not to come back. You may not believe me, but I want you to wait.

'It does not matter. I know. I have spoken.'

VI

Her triumph was real and urgent, but now was no time for indulging it. She walked back to the fire circle as though, from her waiting place apart, she had just seen the counsellors returning. It was time to go to bed; she found her place on the sheepskins inside the hogahn. It was stuffy and warm in there save for a faint draft of air in under the blanket that closed the door and out the smoke-hole, and a coldness that seeped through the ground from outside, where the finger-tips of one hand had touched the floor.

That is how he feels, then. All mine. I can do anything. *Ya,* Wounded Face! Then, if I am so sure of him, why not come to live here? It is dangerous there. What a strange idea: when I am most sure I can do as I want, I give it up. Hunh! We have made almost a thousand dollars in ten months, counting the horses he has now. Everything is going perfectly. George eats out of my hand. I am strong.

She was becoming drowsy and making pictures. There was a story she remembered faintly, how Nayeinezgani did not kill the Hunger People. An allegory; her Slayer of Enemy Gods could not kill them, either. She could do away with them.

I have seen more than you and all you People, I know more. I shall lead you on the trail.

I, Slim Girl, Came With War.

CHAPTER THIRTEEN

I

THEY rode away from T'o Tlakai in gay company —Bay Horse and Bow's Son, Tall Brave from T'ies Napornss and his wife, and half a dozen others, men and women, returning towards T'o Tlikahn, Tsébitai, and Seinsaidesah. It had turned sharply cold, the ponies went well; they played and raced, showing off their jewelry and best clothes and horsemanship—all young people. Bay Horse smoked on a dead twig, blowing out clouds of breath.

'See my new magic! I take this twig, and it is a lighted cigarette.'

'*Ei-yei*, Grandfather; see if you can swallow all your smoke.'

They came to the foot of the slope leading to Gomulli T'o trading post.

A man said, 'Let us go buy some crackers and canned fruit.'

'It's too cold. Some coffee would be good, I think.'

'Maybe Yellow Mustache will give us some,' Laughing Boy said. 'Why did he not come to the dance?'

'Yellow Mustache is not there any longer; he has gone to Chiezb'utso. The man there now is called Narrow Nose.'

'What is he like?'

'He is no good. When we put things in pawn, he sells them before we can buy them back. He is small; inside himself he is small.'

'He tries to be smart with us, but he is not good at it. His word is not good.'

'He thinks we are fools. He ought to look at himself.'

Laughing Boy broke into the chorus of information—'Wait a moment!'

He rode over to Jesting Squaw's Son and whispered in his ear. His friend smiled.

'I am thinking about coffee. I can make him give us all coffee free, I think. Who will bet?'

'I know you,' said Bay Horse, 'I won't.'

Bow's Son whispered to Slim Girl, 'He is like this. They are like this, those two, when they are together. They are not for nothing, their names.'

'I will bet two bits, just to make a bet,' Tall Brave said.

A stranger offered fifty cents. Laughing Boy gave each of them his stake.

'Now, you all go up to the post. Go in. Do not buy, not anything. None of you know me; if any one else is there tell him not to know me; but you all know my grandfather here. You, little sister,' he looked at his wife, 'stay here.'

They rode away while he advised with his friend. Then he explained to Slim Girl, and took her silver bridle. After a slow cigarette he said,

'When that shadow reaches that stick will be time, I think. I go.'

Gomulli T'o trading post stood on a flat, bare shoulder of sand and rock, a level space of half a dozen acres, rising to the west, falling to the east. There was a corral with sides six feet high, and the L-shaped one-story house of stone and adobe with a corrugated iron roof. Around it was nothing green, nothing varied, just sand and rocks, some tin cans, part of a rotted blue shirt. There was no relief. In summer the drenching sun searched out its barren walls; in winter the wind was bleak around it. It was just something dumped there, a thing made by man, contributing nothing, in the midst of majestic desolation. Beyond its level were red-brown cliffs, dull orange bald-rock, yellow sand, leading away to blend into a kind of purplish brown with blue clouds of mountains for background. This did not belong; it was crushed and empty.

Besides the ones belonging to his own party, Laughing Boy noted two other ponies hitched by the corral. He made his fast with a bow-knot, the animal being rather unenterprising and not having learned how to untie them. He looped the reins over the saddle-horn and sauntered to the door of the store, trailing the bridle carelessly, and adjusting his recently acquired hat. It was a stiff-brimmed felt, with the crown undented and the string tied under the chin, Indian fashion, becoming him well. He gave it a wicked slant.

The store was a square room with a counter around three sides; in the fourth the door and a small window. Another door in the back led to the rest of the house. Now the room was rank with tobacco smoke and the heat of an iron stove. The Indians lounged along the counter, leaning on it with their elbows, talking or staring at the goods on the shelves. He recognized the owners of the two ponies—Stinks Like a Mexican, an old rogue with his hair cut short to the level of his ears, who had worked for the railroad, and Long Tooth, the policeman from T'ies Napornss.

He stood in the door.

Bow's Son regarded him blankly.

'Where to, tell?'

'To T'o Tlakai, for the dance.'

'The dance is over; we come from it.'

'*Chiendi!*'

'Where from, tell?' Tall Brave asked.

'Chiziai.'

'That's far!'

'Yes. You tell, where do you live?'

'T'ies Napornss.'

He drifted to the far end, where the trader sat, feet on the counter, chewing listlessly. The man was partly bald, with drooping, pepper-and-salt mustaches and a stupid, narrow face. He looked stingy and ignorant, not bad.

An unsuccessful dry farmer, he had bought a poor post, sight unseen, and come out to make quick money from the ignorant Indians. Somehow it didn't work. They fooled him and exasperated him until he strove frantically to out-cheat them, and that didn't work either. He had no idea of how to attract their trade,

119

nor of how to circumvent their sharpness. It was always like this. Two men had been there since he opened the store in the morning, making one nickel purchase, and now none of these others wanted to buy. They just wanted to talk. They thought he was running a God-damned club.

Laughing Boy sprawled against the counter, clicking a quarter against his teeth. His face was vacuous while he studied the ranks of tin cans. This part came natural to him. He thought idly that it was six months since he had been in a store. It was too bad Yellow Mustache was gone. Yellow Mustache would have welcomed him, and probably given him some candy.

'What kind of candy have you?' He spoke in the baby-talk Navajo that they use with Americans.

'Round-soft-ones,   hard-clear-ones,   and   brown sweets.'

The man was not really at home even in the trade language. He was a little hard of hearing; it hampered him in learning.

'How much are the round-soft-ones?'

'Two for a yellow.'

Laughing Boy examined his change carefully, and put a dime on the counter. 'Give me a blue's worth.'

The trader let four gum drops roll toward the customer. 'Give it to me.' He reached for the dime.

Laughing Boy held onto it. 'Haven't you any twisted-sticks?'

'No.'

'I don't want those.' He put his money back in his pocket. 'Give me a smoke.'

Narrow Nose eyed him for a moment, as though he would like to see him shrivel. Policy was policy. He slid a half-empty sack of Stud and some papers along the counter.

'Match, brother-in-law.'

'You have some.' He pointed to the Indian's shirt pocket.

'I need those.'

'Well, you go to hell!' Narrow Nose swore in English with that fatuous confidence of not being understood.

"*Juthla hago ni*," Laughing Boy paraphrased softly, half as though interpreting to himself, half as though
120

throwing it back. The insult, in Navajo, is serious. There was a laugh.

He lolled against the counter, lit his cigarette, and puffed at it critically.

'I think I buy that saddle. Let me see it.'

'I'll take it down if you really want it.'

It hung from a rafter, among other saddles, quirts, bridles, pots, Pendleton blankets, ropes, silk handkerchiefs, and axes.

'Let me see it. My saddle is worn out. I need a new one. I want that blanket there, I think, and four red cans of tobacco, the kind with the preacher in the long black coat on it.'

'Can you pay for all that?'

'I give this in pawn.'

He clanked the bridle onto the counter. Stinks Like a Mexican drew nearer.

'I want that handkerchief there, I think.' He nodded toward a silk one. 'And a knife that shuts.'

The trader got up, feigning reluctance. The way the man had made up his mind to buy was typical. He hefted the bridle—ninety to a hundred dollars. Things were looking up. If he got his hooks in this, in return for thirty dollars' worth of goods—

'Where do you live?'

'Chiziai.'

'Where's that?'

'Down there.'

Indians edged up to handle the silver. Narrow Nose turned to the policeman, who spoke a little English.

'Where's Chiziai?'

'Lo Palo. Mebbe-so laillload tlack side him sit down. Him come flom dere now, me sabbey.' He didn't quite know what was up, but he wasn't going to spoil it.

'Los Palos, hunh? I know.'

'I came up for the dance, now I go back. In Eagles' Young Moon I shall come back and take out my bridle.'

That sounded good. Five—six months, likely he'd forget it. Likely it wouldn't be here.

'Is he speaking true?' The trader asked the store in general.

Bow's Son held up the bridle. 'This is the kind of work they do down there. It is not like the work up

121

here, not like my father's jewelry,' he lied. Bay Horse and Tall Brave agreed. Narrow Nose knew them and Two Bows well. He believed them.

'Good, I take your bridle.' He reached for it, wanting to feel its possession.

'Wait a moment; put down the goods.'

He assembled them laboriously. 'Forty-one dollars and one blue.'

'How?'

'Saddle, twenty-seven; blanket, ten—thirty-seven; tobacco, six blues; handkerchief, two dollars; knife, twelve bits; forty-one dollars and one blue. I make it forty-one dollars.'

Laughing Boy strung out the bargaining stubbornly, until he heard singing outside. The trader had stuck at thirty-five dollars.

'Good, I take them.'

He started to push over the bridle; Narrow Nose had his fingers on the heavy silver. Jesting Squaw's Son and Slim Girl entered together.

'*Ahalani!*'

'*Ahalani, shichai!*'

The two men strode up to each other, Laughing Boy still clutching the harness. The trader's hands felt empty. They hugged each other, wrestled, went through a huge pantomime of friendship.

'It is good to see you, my friend!'

'Very much it is good to see you!'

'*Hozhoni!*'

'*Aigisi hozhoni!*'

'What are you doing here?'

'I came up for the dance, but I am too late, they say. What are your news?'

'I have just got married. This is my wife, she comes from Maito.'

'Good!'

Narrow Nose thought he must be progressing in the language, he could understand most of what they said. Usually when they talked among themselves, he could not follow, they seemed to mess it around so. He had no idea that they were using baby-talk for his special benefit, any more than it occurred to him as unusual that a man should be bringing a bride to live in his settlement, instead of going to hers.

Jesting Squaw's Son shook hands with his other friends there, as though he had just come back from a trip.

'I have just finished building our hogahn, over towards T'ies Napornss. We are going to make the House Prayer in a little while. I want you all to come now, we shall make a feast afterwards. You, my friend, you must come. Come now.'

He nodded at Tall Brave, who started to the door with a couple of the others.

'But I am making a trade here. I must finish it.'

'You can make a better trade with the trader at T'ies Napornss. He is a good man.'

Narrow Nose swore to himself. He wanted that bridle, and he wanted that new couple's custom. Jesting Squaw was well-to-do; she would give her son plenty of sheep.

'I give you a good trade. Stay here and finish it.'

'I go with my friend to feast, I think. All these people are going.'

'Yes,' Tall Brave struck in from the doorway, 'it is time to eat.'

'Why don't you buy food and feast here?'

'I have food there, coffee and meat and bread. Why should they buy food here?' Jesting Squaw's Son told him.

The trader made a quick calculation, involving about a dollar and a quarter.

'I will give you coffee and crackers and some canned plums. How is that?'

'*Ei-yei!* Then we shall stay.'

'He must be a good man to deal with,' Laughing Boy said solemnly.

Narrow Nose called through the back door,

'Make about three quarts of coffee, quick, and put jest a little sweetnin' in it. Bring out ten cups.' He set out two boxes of saltines and four cans of plums. 'Now, give me the bridle.'

'I think I get something more, a rope, perhaps. You are a good man to buy from.' He laid the bridle on the counter, but hung onto the reins.

Narrow Nose climbed onto the counter and pulled down a length of rope. 'This is good.'

'No, I want horsehair.' With his mouth full.

'No horsehair.'

'Rawhide, then.'

He had to search under the counter for hide ropes that Indians had made. Laughing Boy went over them minutely. The coffee came. The Indians wolfed down the food and drink, and tipped up the cans to drain the fruit juice.

Laughing Boy said, before he had swallowed his last mouthful,

'I do not think I want those things.'

'Hunh?'

Drawing at the reins, he made the bridle seem to walk off the counter.

'Hey, stop!'

He turned at the door. 'Another time, perhaps.'

'Hey, by Gawd!'

All the Indians streamed out, with the trader after them. Laughing Boy was off at a gallop, his wife and Jesting Squaw's Son close behind. The rest followed, whooping and swinging their ropes and whips. Narrow Nose stood in the sand.

'Hey!'

Inside the store, Stinks Like a Mexican collected some tobacco and a handkerchief. He slid through the door, and vanished around the corner of the house.

'God damn a red devil!'

The Indians went fast; already their singing was distant. It was cold. He stuck his hands into his pockets and stared after them.

'God damn a red son of a bitch!'

CHAPTER FOURTEEN

I

IT began to snow on the morning of the third day of their trip home, not far from Kintiel. The ground, where it had any dampness in it, had been frozen since the night before, and they had hurried under a threatening sky, having still a good day's ride before them. The storm came down like timber-wolves, rushing. A mountain-top wind sent the dry flakes whirling past, stinging their ears and the sides of their faces; there was no sun, they could see only a few yards ahead of them. Pulling their blankets up over their heads, they guided themselves by the wind at their backs.

An Indian takes the weather passively, accepting and enduring it without the European's mental revolt or impatience. Comfort and fat living had changed this to some degree in Laughing Boy; he was unusually aware of discomfort, and resentful, rating the blizzard as colder than it was. Slim Girl was simply miserable. They did not speak, but jogged on, punishing their horses.

Time passed and the wind slackened, so that the snow about their ponies' hooves stayed still, although the fall of flakes continued. Laughing Boy was preoccupied with thoughts of the road, but his wife contrasted this ride with the other time when they had ridden this way together. First it is the top of a stove and then it is an ice-machine, she thought; yet I am beginning to love it.

Cliffs loomed before them, duskily blue with snowflakes rebounding and zigzagging before they touched the rock. The snow was beginning to drift.

'These are not the right cliffs,' he said; 'the wind must have shifted, I think. I was afraid it would.'

'What shall we do, then?'

'I think this is Inaiyé Cletso'i; we follow to the left.'

'Why not camp here?'

'We must find firewood. We might just sleep here and not wake up. Come along, little sister, perhaps we shall find a hogahn.'

They continued, he fully occupied, she miserable with nothing to do save follow. Sometimes the snow whirled up at them, sometimes a flaw would sting their faces with fine, white dust. Their heavy blankets felt thin as cotton over their shoulders.

'There's a hogahn.' She pushed forward.

'*Hogay-gahn,* bad. Do not stop here!'

'What do you mean?'

'Don't you see it is deserted? Don't you see the hole in the north side? Some one has died here. Come along.'

She sighed in anger, gritted her teeth, swore under her breath, and turned her horse back. Nothing on earth would make a Navajo stop there; he would not even use the dry timbers for firewood to save his life. Well, it was part of the rest.

'We are coming somewhere now,' he called to her.

"How?'

'I smell smoke. There, you can see.'

It was a well-built hut beside a corral. Smoke issued from the hole in the roof. The dome of daubed mud and untrimmed logs looked beautiful just then. Laughing Boy shouted at the door, and a middle-aged man crawled out.

'Where are you going?'

'To Chiziai.'

'You are out of the trail; it is far.'

'This snow confused us.'

'Where from?'

'T'o Tlakai.'

'Where's that?'

'Between Seinsaidesah and Agathla.'

'*Ei-yei!* You come far! Just beyond, there, is a box

126

cañon. There is shelter and feed. Put your horses there, Grandfather. Drop your saddles here, I shall bring them in. Come in, Grandmother.'

They lost no time over the horses, and crawled gladly into the smoky, fetid, warm hogahn. There were the man, two women, four children between eight and fifteen, and two dogs. The space was a circle some twelve feet in diameter—the average size; with the people, the fire in the middle, saddles, cooking utensils, a loom and blankets, it was well filled.

'You live at T'o Tlakai?'

'No, at Chiziai. My parents live there. There was a Night Chant; for that we went. It was a full ten days' chant. Mountain Singer conducted it.'

'Beautiful!'

'Yes.'

The elder wife served them a pot of boiled mutton and corn, with a chunk of the usual tough wheat bread. They ate readily. It flashed through Laughing Boy's mind that he had not enjoyed a meal so much since his arrival at Tsé Lani, but then he thought that that was silly. The foods to which he was accustomed!

II

They were storm-bound for all the next day. He was anxious to be home again, now that the restraint of the ceremony and after-ceremony was ended. He wanted to have Slim Girl to himself, at leisure, and to enjoy their own special kind of life once more. So he was impatient and ready to find fault.

It was a long time since he had been confined in a winter hogahn, with its crowded things and people and close-packed smells. Their house at Los Palos was always aired. At T'o Tlakai it still had been warm enough to leave the door unblanketed during the day, and he had spent most of his time in the brush-walled medicine-lodge. He found it too close here, and was made self-conscious by fearing what she might think of it.

The modern Navajo diet, boiled mutton and tough bread, tough bread and boiled mutton, a little corn and squash, coffee with not enough sugar, tea as black as coffee, had none of the delicacy of the old ceremonial dishes. He went outside only on rising, when they all rolled in the snow (it had never occurred to him to warn Slim Girl of that custom, but she followed suit without a sign), and again for half an hour to look at his ponies. The thick air inside weighed upon him; he felt dull after a heavy breakfast, and had no more appetite.

Then there were the lice. His wife had rid him of them, conquering his sincere belief that they were a gift from Old Couple in the World Below to enable people to sleep. He had rated that as one of her minor magics. No new ones had got on to him at T'o Tlakai, but in this crowded place they stormed him. He was not used to being bitten, so he was tormented, and he scratched a great deal.

His host asked him naïvely, 'You have many lice, Grandfather?'

He caught his tongue in time, answering, 'No, but they nearly froze yesterday. Now they have waked up again, and they are hungry.'

Slim Girl gave him a look of approval and sympathy, with a little gesture of scratching furiously at herself. He smiled.

The afternoon and early evening were better, for his host recounted the second part of the Coming Up story to his children, the part about the Twin Gods, Slayer of Enemy Gods, and Child of the Waters, which Laughing Boy loved best. He noticed that Slim Girl listened intently. Some day he would be telling his children. It seemed a long time for them not to have had any, but he really did not know very much about these things. It was the woman's business; the children were hers, after all. She would arrange it in due time, according to her wisdom. He drowsed and was soothed by the tale of the familiar, strange adventures, the gate of the Clashing Rocks, the trail over Boiling Sands, Monster Eagle and Monster Elk and Big God, lightning-arrows and cloud-blankets. After supper the close air drugged him; his eyes were nearly closed as he listened to the last of the myth.

The snowflakes, drifting through the smoke-hole, fell into the fire with little hisses. The even voice went on, telling the end.

'Slayer of Enemy Gods came to the Hunger People they say . . .'

But it was not his dream, there was nothing portentous about this voice. Slim Girl had slain the Hunger People. He smiled and listened, cradled in drowsiness, distantly conscious of a louse biting him, and comforting himself with the thought that to-morrow all that would be attended to, to-morrow they would be home again. These poor people, they could not know. He half-opened his eyes, seeing his wife's thoughtful, delicate face, and said, as sleepy people will, much louder than he realized,

'Hasché Lto'i!'

'What was that, Grandfather?' asked the man.

'Nothing.'

'I thought you said something about Hunting Goddness.'

'No, I said "hashké yei itei," the gods are brave.'

'Unh! That is well said.'

Slim Girl reflected. Hashché Lto'i was one of the few real goddesses, but she had nothing at all to do with the Coming Up story. He had covered his slip neatly, that man of hers. He was no child. They two would go far, far, under her direction.

The story-telling ended, and the flakes had ceased falling through the smoke-hole. To-morrow would be clear. The banked fire became a dull redness, scarcely glowing.

III

They covered the fifteen miles home at a racing pace, on a morning of clear, brilliant air and dry, fresh snow. They both felt glorious, released from the cramped hogahn, glad to be approaching their goal. Though she had no great endurance, Slim Girl rode well, and now, with their ponies prancing in the cold, played tricks and frolicked on horseback as Indian men and women rarely do together. They both yipped and waved their arms; she snatched his hat, and threw it for him to pick from the ground on the run; he swung low under his pony's neck and sent an arrow skimming ahead of them. Before they reached it, the special quality and privacy of their home reached out to them, and they were almost definitely conscious of reëntering their own way of living as though one entered an enclosure.

He admired anew the fireplace, with its smokelessness, its draft that set the flame quickly blazing, the heat thrown out from its shallow back. She prepared food while he tended to the ponies. The house became warm, but the air was sweet, the adobe walls and clay floor were clean, and now, with lively appetites, they smelt the good food cooking. She sat back from the fire while things stewed and bubbled. Kneeling beside her, he kissed her—to him perhaps more than anything else the act symbolic of their life apart—and they smiled at each other with grave pleasure. For a minute she was limp in his arms, then she pushed him away with an affectionate, scolding word and returned to a pot that was boiling over. He lay back on the sheepskins, watching. Domesticity, his wife, his home, perfection.

The loom-frame hung near the door; on the other side was the anvil. The place was permeated with an excited happiness, fulness, completion. Had any religious-minded Navajo, sensitive enough to the reiterated doctrine of *hozoji* to feel it without words, entered that place, he would have felt that he had, indeed, entered the 'house of happiness.'

CHAPTER FIFTEEN

I

The winter passed as swiftly as the summer; more so, in fact, for, feeling more sure of herself, Slim Girl consented to a social life. They went to various dances, becoming better known among the Southern Navajos, who began to accept her as entirely one of themselves. Learning with practice better and better how to avoid being different in a way that troubled others, she was able to be one of them without the fatal appearance of serve and effort. By a slow process, she saw, Laughing Boy really was bringing her back into her own people. She consented out of policy to undergo the Night Chant initiation, the scourging with yucca leaves, the demonstration of the masks, and having done so found, surprised at her own naïveté, that it was a genuine source of satisfaction to her. Knowing that something of the true substance was forever lost to her, she surrounded herself as much as possible with the trappings of Navajo-ism.

There were obstacles and interruptions: a double life carries heavy enough penalties, and a past is a past, particularly if its locale is much the same as that of the present. Red Man, the wrestler of Tsé Lani, sophisticated and self-willed, was present at many of those dances. Slim Girl had never given him more than hope, and even that, he felt, more because he served a purpose than for anything else. She had used him. Now she belonged to this rustic, who had humiliated him, and who obviously did not know what it was all about. Red Man was too good an Indian to bear much resentment for the wrestling defeat, but it served the purpose of preventing him from amusing himself by explaining to Laughing Boy just what he knew about his wife. Besides, he shrewdly suspected, such a recital would be dangerous in the extreme.

So he adopted an attitude of smiling implications, of 'I could and I would' that was as effective as possible for making trouble. Laughing Boy remembered the dancing at Tsé Lani, and he felt distrubed. Watching Red Man, it came upon him that, remarkable though his wife was, she was subject to the same general laws as other people, and he was fairly sure that he was not the first man she had known in love. Many things suddenly aligned themselves in a new way to assume a monstrous form. He became very quiet, and thought hard.

Slim Girl saw it immediately, not knowing what he was thinking, but feeling the reality of her peril. At that dance, she paid no attention to it, continued as ever, and treated Red Man with cool friendliness. At home, she managed to bring him into the talk, told Laughing Boy how he had sought to marry her once, and described with entire truth an ugly scene with him at Tsé Lani. Her husband listened, and was gladly convinced.

Her past was her past, he thought; he knew enough of her to know that it had been more than unhappy, and that she had put it resolutely behind her. There was much suffering, many bad things, of which she never spoke. Some day, perhaps, she could tell him. In any case, he believed what she did say, and even had the case been otherwise, that was all dead.

The next time they met, he contemplated the man, and guessed at the dimensions of his soul. Taking an opportunity when they both were taking horses to water, he rode up beside him, sitting sideways on his bare-backed pony, one hand on the mane, one hand on the rump—a casual pose for a careless chat. Red Man greeted him non-committally.

'Grandfather, let us not run around things, let us not pretend,' he said. 'You have not said anything, but you have said too much. Do not pretend not to know what I mean. If you like what you are doing so much that you are willing to fight about it, go on. If not, stop it. I say, not just do less of it, or do it differently, but stop it entirely. That is what I mean. I have spoken.'

Red Man studied him; he was plainly in deadly earnest. He might just as well have acted instead of spoken—those men from up there have not yet realized the power of police and law. Among Navajos, the reasonable and acceptable way to have done, had he acted, would have been from ambush. Red Man felt he had had a narrow escape. He emphatically did not like what he was doing that much. Time would inevitably bring sorrow to the fellow.

'I hear you, Grandfather.'

II

These occasional absences of from three days to over a week made complications in Slim Girl's arrangements with her American. His trips in to town from his ranch were made on business that was, as often as not, conjured up to excuse himself to himself for seeing her. Each rendezvous would be arranged the time before, or by a note left in the little house, which she was supposed to visit at fixed intervals. Now it was occurring, as never before, that he would demand her presence on a certain date, only to be told it was impossible. Increasingly, as her love for her husband gained upon her, he suspected part of the truth, and tormented himself with jealousy. That husband, whom he had always regarded as rather mythical, seemed in the past few months to have become exacting. In moments of honesty towards himself, he writhed at the acid thought of being used by a squaw for the benefit of herself and some low, presumably drunken, Indian.

He rode into Los Palos through the bottomless mud and wet of a spring thaw, only to find a note on the table:

DEAR GEORGE

My husband make me go too dance I will come day after tomorrow afternoon. pleas not mind.

love

LILLIAN

The poor fool cursed, got drunk, and waited over.

That had been a very pleasant dance; they had ridden part of the way home with as likable a crowd as the one that rode from T'o Tlakai to the trading post. She still tasted the flavour of it as she changed into her Sears-Roebuck dress and set out for Los Palos. Laughing Boy had surprised on her face, once or twice, that look of triumphant hatred when she returned. He would have been astonished could he have seen her now.

She looked back on their house, on the corral and the still leafless young peach trees, visualizing the dance, her people, and him. Her face was tender, almost yearning. Then she turned away towards the town, and braced her shoulders. For a moment she smiled, a war-path smile, and she was hard. Her upper lip curled back, showing her small, even, white teeth. Then her expression was blank; that passive look upon her oval face that made one turn to it again and again, wondering what deep, strong thoughts were going on behind the lovely mask.

He was in the house before her. She braced herself again at the door, then blotted everything from her eyes, becoming a happy, pretty woman with nothing on her mind. He rose as she entered. He did not answer her smile or move to touch her; that meant there would be a scene. Oh, well!

'Look here, Lillian, this is getting too thick. Here I come in here just to see you—we made the date, didn't we?—and you've gone prancing off to some dance. It won't do. I don't ask so much of you, but you've got to keep your dates, do you see? Don't make me suspect you . . .'

She hated scenes, loud voices, turmoil, protestations. God damn this man. *Juthla hago hode shonk*. She sat still, looking at him with wide, hurt eyes and drooping mouth. By and by he ran down.

'You tink lak dat about me! You tink I forget everything! What for you tink dose tings, hey? I'm sorry I go away. I do it because I got to, you see? My husban', he tink someting bad, I tink. So he act mean, dat man. But you know.'

'The trouble is I don't know. I wonder about you. I wonder if you try at all, or just do what's handiest for you. I've got some consideration coming to me, you know.'

The man was truly jealous, he was miserable, she had him right in the palm of her hand. She didn't have to say much, just let him do it. After he'd got rid of all this, the fact remained that he loved her, and that was all that mattered.

He drew her towards him, she sat on his knees, her hands on his shoulders. he bent her face back and stared into her eyes. They were deep, deep, and swimming. There was a look in them that thrilled him, a look that must be true. Now there was an imprint of real truth in her words and gestures, and the fierceness of her kiss.

She was not acting any loner, she did not have to pretend this. There was no more falseness in it than there is in an arrow leaving a bow. She hated him. On him she had concentrated all her feelings towards Americans in general, every thing that she had ever suffered. In him she was revenging herself upon them all. Her kisses were weapons, her tendernesses were blows struck in the full heat of battle. She was revenging herself, and she was acquiring the means to her perfect life.

Bound by those hours of happiness, he could not break away. These days, he gave her more money than he ever had before, more than he could well afford, seeking to bind her to him, knowing that that was no way to arrive at truth, but craving, if she were lying to him, to be lied to so well he would be convinced. He made many efforts to improve her, feeling how remarkable a woman she was. He wanted her to read books, but her distaste for them was deep and sincere; he wanted to make a superior American out of her. He would have liked to raise her to a position in which he could respect himself if he married her.

She was afraid always that he would ask her that, but he was not quite so lost. She kept him at tension, administering happiness and unhappiness carefully, accepted his increased gifts, and in her mind shortened the time of waiting. But it did not make a smooth road to travel.

III

She was beset by difficulties and entanglements, but she was conquering them one by one, even turning them to her use, as though she were taking weapons from her enemies. She could shape and bend men, she could control her destinies in theirs. In her thoughts, she tasted in advance the happiness of the goal towards which she aimed, and she felt her power, power, power; and so, as far as she could tell, she was happy.

Her weaving was winning Laughing Boy's unstinted praise, and, to her surprise and great satisfaction, becoming a source of income. The trading post in Los Palos would pass on to her occasional orders from tourists or people in the East. If she had been willing to weave the entirely un-Indian pictures of actual objects that so many tourists demand, she could have had all the work she could handle at fancy prices; but she refused to do anything, or use any colours not purely Navajo, and she strengthened her husband in his natural reluctance to stamp shapeless strings of swasti-kas, thunder-birds, and other curiosities on his silver. She was precious about it, as she was about all Nava-jo things. It was one piece with her eagerness to speak familiarly of everything familiar to them, to participate in every phase of their life, to acquire completely the Navajo gesture. When they were rich and lived in the North, she thought, she would make herself an in-fluence for preserving all native ways; she would use any power they acquired in combating Christianity, short hair, shoes, ready-made trousers, and the creep-ing in of American-derived words. Already she had amused her husband by insisting on calling coffee by its old, cumbrous name of little-split-round-ones, instead of the much easier 'coghwé,' that had been taken into the language.

Laughing Boy's reputation was spreading. The Har-vey agent had made her a tentative offer for them to come to Grand Cañon. In the beginning of spring, at planting time, they moved forge and loom outdoors again. At sunset, laying aside tools, or coming in, tired and at peace, from working in the soft earth, they sang together.

Now was the time when ponies began to grow fat, and the desert was all one mass of flowers. Remember-ing a good thing from her school days, Slim Girl brought in great bunches, Indian paint brush, fireweed, cactus blooms, and a hundred others, and stuck them in tin cans about the house. This puzzled Laughing Boy at first, but later he caught on, and enjoyed grouping them, with a good feeling for arrangements of masses of colour, but little interest in the blossoms as such.

There was movement in the desert. Horse-trading picked up again. The first sprouts of corn came through the ground, the peach trees began to put out leaves; one of them triumphantly produced a blossom. The days slipped by. Life was settled, serene, mo-notonous; there was no detail of it that one would wish to change.

CHAPTER SIXTEEN

I

Any married couple, no matter how perfect the match, will undergo a critical period of strain, and these two were no exception. For all the dances, winter was a hemmed-in time; repetitious days indoors were a searching test of companionship. Slim Girl went into town, Laughing Boy sallied forth to watch over the herd; but they moved out of the home atmosphere together only for those eight or nine ceremonies.

They were attempting a difficult thing. They needed not only to see occasional outsiders when they were apart, new faces made attractive by the mere fact that they break the sameness, but also the presence of a third person when they were together, that their solitude might retain its value. and their unity refresh itself from the sense of the outsider's foreignness.

This same life, so closely together, will make people unusually sensitive to each other's moods; sometimes, if they are fond of each other, almost morbidly so. He did not answer that question; perhaps he thinks it was stupid. She handed me that cup of coffee abruptly; perhaps I have offended her in something.

They came through it remarkably well, and still deeply in love. But Slim Girl, watching her husband with close attention, felt him change and was troubled. Feeling less sure of herself, she was over-careful, and betrayed more than ever that reserve of something withheld that belonged inevitably to her double life. Each increased the other's uneasiness; it was a circle.

He did not read himself. The melting snows refreshed the pasturage, the grass grew tall. He gathered his scattered horses, shifted them, and watched them fatten. His peach trees grew, his corn was well above the sand. All these were good things, and in each he rejoiced as he enjoyed each detail of his day, the far riding and the loom before the house door, his wife's talk, the ring of his hammer. Each thing was good, and yet the whole was dull and devoid of savour.

Laughing Boy knew well enough that people wore on each other, and that every couple underwent a period of adjustment. He knew that in many households, when the man became seriously restless, his first wife would arrange for him to take a second to preserve the home. But such was hardly the case here. He was by habit one who faced issues squarely and thought them out tough-mindedly, but now in the back of his head were many thoughts, safely hidden from himself, from which unease, like an infection, flowed through his system.

He did not realize that he was studying his wife critically, as one might an opponent. Once or twice, to his own surprise, he caught himself about to become annoyed with her over little or nothing; once or twice, away from her, building up a quite unreasonable sense of wrong. Then he would be disgusted with himself, and alarmed. The process was really natural enough; being profoundly dissatisfied with something in her which he refused to recognize, the feeling sought to give itself outlet by picking causes of annoyance which could be admitted.

She had always foreseen a period of difficulty and settling down, and was prepared to adapt herself to it, but now she did not know what was needed. She thought she was sophisticated, she thought she knew all about men, and all about herself. She thought she had penetrated to the ultimate truth. She knew only a little of life, not all of herself, and of men there was a half which she knew through and through, and a half which she was just beginning to discover. She wondered if the time had come at last to give up her American and go North. But this was a bad year for them; wool, and hence the sheep which they would have to buy, had risen, while horses, blankets, and jewelry sold badly.

The tourists were unusually few. And here she had her one sure source of income.

Then she had a fatal thought. She was learning, from herself and from laughing Boy, how much more there is to love than what is covered by its lowest terms. She was thinking things out by herself—particularly when she was weaving—like a philosopher. With the realization of the other things that are needed to make love worthy of itself, the bare fact that her husband and herself were in love with each other ceased to be sufficient. She wondered if, by falling in love when she had thought to make a deliberate choice, she had really known what she was doing. She wondered if life with this man, who was sometimes silent and strange, sometimes stupid, and sometimes irritating, might not be dismal in that wild homeland of his.

She did not really believe in her own doubt; it was purely an intellectual concept; but the dominant motive in her life for so many years had been the determination to move coolly towards a predetermined, sure success. Had she studied Napoleon in that California school, she would have admired him, and she might have been warned by him. Now, looking back on her past triumphs, she decided to wait until she made surely sure. Just a few months more, a year at the most, and George was making a lot of money in sheep. Some of that would come in handy.

II

As summer approached, Laughing Boy became restless and more worried at his own condition. Had he offended a god, he wondered. He took a sweat-bath, sang, and tried a fast. It did not seem to make much difference

He made up his mind one morning when he was leaving to round up three ponies for sale. Slim Girl had seemed abstracted; he had noticed her watching him curiously, seeming nervous. She had been like that various times lately, yet what could he say about it? It was just an impression. He felt sullen, snapped at her. Her hurt surprise made him miserable. As he mounted his horse, he thought, 'I must surely find a singer.'

There could be no doubt that he had done some

unconscious wrong, deserting the trail of Beauty. Forces of evil were preying upon him, he was no longer immune from bad thoughts. Stated in the American idiom, he decided he must be sick.

It was the merest chance that he met Yellow Singer walking along the trail with a bundle over his shoulder. Laughing Boy debated consulting him, and decided against it: not that ugly man.

'*Ahalani*, Grandfather,' the medicine man called to him; 'wait a minute.'

'*Ahalani*, Grandfather, I wait.'

The old rogue was standing straight and walking briskly; one saw that he was a tall man. Laughing Boy smelled whiskey.

'I see that you need medicine, little brother.'

'Unh! Why do you think that?'

Yellow Singer noted the grunt and followed his lead. 'I dreamed last night that when you were at the dance at Buckho Dotklish, you put those prayer cigarettes wrong. They fell down into the sand. Now they have put a spider's web into your brain.'

'You are right. I am not well.'

He nodded wisely. 'So I went and got the remedy for you. I am ready to make you all right. You are a good young man; it will be my pleasure to make you all right.' He glowed with benevolence.

Evidently this man had more power than one would think. 'How much will you want?'

'Twenty dollars.'

Laughing Boy considered. It was not a high fee. He counted out six dollars in coin, and pulled three plaques from his silver belt. 'There, that is really worth more.'

The old man hefted the metal. 'All right.'

'What must I do?'

'You must go to a place alone, you must wash your hair. Then pray to the Divine Ones whose cigarettes you offended. Then take this remedy.'

Out of the bundle he took a bottle of red liquor, looked at it a moment, and then, benevolence conquering, took out a second and handed them over.

'What is this?'

'It is a special kind of whiskey. It is very holy. The

140

Americans drink it; it is so good they try to keep any one else from having it.'

'How do I take it?'

'When you have prayed, just start drinking it. By and by you will feel your mind becoming all right, your heart will be high. Then you will sleep. When you wake up, you will feel badly, but if you take some more, you will feel all right. One bottle should be enough. Put the other away until something tells you you need it.'

'I see.'

'I shall go on the trail to Buckho Dotklish, and make a charm there, to prevent any more bad things coming to you from those cigarettes. Tell no one about this, above all no woman. It is very holy and secret, if you speak of it, it will do you harm. It will make you jump into the fire.'

'I see.'

'If you need more, let me know. I may be able to get you some.'

He rode to his usual camping place by Natahne-tinn, and went solemnly about the prescribed ceremonial. Then he tasted the drink. It was unlike the white whiskey; not so bad, but still pretty bad—low-grade, frontier tanglefoot rye, dear at a dollar a bottle.

After the first few drinks it came easier, but it did not make him feel very happy. As he grew drunk, he longed more and more for his own country, and for a truce from the constant feeling of the presence of alien things. About the time it grew dark, he stopped drinking and walked up and down. At first he sang, then he was silent.

Liquor, taken in solitude, sometimes has this effect. Along with a megalomaniac sense of his central position in the universe, a man grows bluntly honest with himself. All the secret, forgotten, stifled thoughts come out of the closet in his mind, and he must face them in turn, without a saving sense of proportion. This now was Laughing Boy's portion.

I am not happy in the house at Chiziai. It is too lonely, too strange a life; no one ever comes. We see people only at dances. That American town, what is there there? What is this preacher's wife? The look in her

141

face when she returns—I do not know. There is something wrong, always something hidden. She is always hiding something. Let us go North, go North, to T'o Tlakai! Oh, my mother!

When I told her about her weaving; when we rode together that time, then she needed me, then I, too, was strong. We were happiest then, both of us. She is stronger; it is she who leads me.

I am afraid to speak to her.

He stopped short and clutched his hands together.

Why? I am afraid to lose her. Am I losing myself? Oh, I do not know, I do not know; this life she has had, this wisdom of hers. What went on before? Who was the man, and what does Red Man know? Perhaps if I spoke to her, she would say no. She makes her own life. I am losing myself. And I cannot leave her, Came With War, Came With War. Oh, no, can't leave her. She would say 'No,' and I should say 'All right,' and then I should be dead.

How long will it be before we are rich enough to suit her? Why will she not herd sheep? All women do. I do not know. This American life she has led, she will not leave such things. It is my enemy. Our life is not good enough for her.

She wants so much money. A year, another year, who knows? So long, long. When will there be children? We should have had children. I want children. I want to go home. What is happening to me? I am losing myself. She holds the reins and I am becoming a led horse. Two, three years, all like this, and Sings Before Spears, who was a warrior, will have ended, and there will just be that part of a man which worships a woman. Not the rest of him, just heat. A bowstring without a bow. Only good for a woman to tie something with.

I need some more medicine.

Another stiff drink sent him over the borderline into incoherent plans for performing wonders. Three or four more put him to sleep.

He was in pretty bad shape when he awoke, late, with the high sun beating upon him. He went down to the arroyo and dabbled in its shallow, unfresh water. He was not as sick as the other time, but he was sick.

'When you wake up, you will feel badly, but if then you take a little more, you will feel all right.'

He would try it. The smell made him feel worse. He poured some into a cup, returned to the arroyo and weakened it with water. Then he downed it in one straining gulp. He did feel better. Perhaps he might take a little more, he thought, reaching for the bottle, and paused with it half-tipped for pouring.

No. He was remembering last night, and that had been terrible. He put it down, and stared at the ashes of his fire.

'Coffee,' he said aloud.

He drank a lot more water when he went to fill his pot. The heat of the flames was unpleasant to him; he was beginning to feel badly again, and wanted a drink. He put a lot of coffee in.

That had been all true, what he had thought last night, but incomplete and exaggerated. He was home-sick, he was afraid of losing her, but what kind of man could not wait a few years, three at the worst, for so reasonable a cause. She was wise, she was right, and he was sure she loved him. Well, then?

The whiskey now, this magic. It did drive the clouds out of his thoughts, but it made everything appear twisted.

He lifted the coffee off the fire. It was strong. Without waiting for the sugar, he tried to drink it, burning his tongue.

It was not magic. It was just something like jimpson-weed. Under its influence he had seen himself, but there was nothing holy about it. He remembered quite clearly how he had placed those cigarettes in a crevice in the rock. There had been nothing wrong about it. That old coyote had made a lucky guess, and followed it up with lies to make money, that was all.

He saw a very clear picture of Yellow Singer and his wife as he had first met them, sober, and reaching for the bottle; he saw other scarecrow Indians he had met in this American's country. He looked at them, and behind them saw incoherently the great, ominous cloud of the American system, something for which he had no name or description.

That was another thing about which Slim Girl had been right, that drink. She knew how to tame it. She had the secret of how to prevent American knowledge from doing harm; she made it serve a good purpose.

He set down his cup of coffee, picked up a rock, and deliberately smashed the bottle. The liquid ran into the coals of the fire, caught, and for a moment the dampened sand burnt with a blue flame. That startled him. To drink something like that! He threw in the fragments of the bottle, in the bottom of which were still a few drops, and watched the blue light flicker briefly above them.

He drank another cup of coffee, with sugar, then unearthed the second bottle from its cache. That had cost money, much money. Well, he'd had his money's worth. From now on he could think without the help of blue flames. He poured it over the fire, and the drenching put the fire out. Eh! This was strange stuff!

To try to round up horses seemed out of the question. He stretched out in the shade of the rocks, craving sleep, his limbs feeling as though he had been through a furious wrestling bout. The sky was too blue, it hurt his eyes; the circling of a distant buzzard made his head ache. He turned over and fixed his gaze on a crack, studying it, sleepy, yet unable to keep his eyes shut.

Yellow Singer and all his kind were bad. They were like an offensive smell. But a smell came from a carcass. Those people were the way they were because of the Americans. The town of Los Palos in the drenching sunlight, quiet, deadlooking beside its irrigated fields. What was it? Something in the air, something that perverted the world. Where they were was no place for Earth People. They had done something to Slim Girl, one could see that, but she seemed to have risen above it. But they were bad for her, too. It was beyond him.

He smoked, and at length slept fitfully through the noonday heat, wakened now and again by flies, to drowse delightfully and return to sleep. In the late evening he went to where a waterfall in the arroyo made a trickling shower bath. The water refreshed him; he was hungry once more, and felt better.

What he had thought last night had been true, but unbalanced; and all this about Americans had been just because he felt sick. He had always known Americans, traders and such, they were all right, just people of a different tribe. He stretched out, fed, smoking, sur-

144

prised at his desire to sleep again. It would be pleasant, it would be beautiful, returning to T'o Tlakai rich, very rich, with her, and to settle down somewhere near there and have children. They needed children. Meantime they would make their way together. Oh, beautiful.

III

Next morning he felt better. The drunknness and the emotional outburst had cleared his system. In pouring out the liquor, he felt that he had destroyed a bad thing; the enemies in his head had indeed proved to be nothing but cobwebs, and they were gone. Like the man who burned the tumbleweed when the Eagles were afraid of it, he thought.

He rounded up the three horses he wanted, good ones. Only the best horses sold this year, and they did not bring so good a price. He rode home contented, quiet, and determined to do better himself.

He found his wife waiting before the door.

'I did not know you were going to be gone so long; I have been lonely without you. Bring in your saddle while I get supper. I am glad when you come back.

'I am always glad to be back.'

'As long as you feel like that, I shall continue to be happy.'

Why should he worry himself about this woman? And why should he worry about anything else as long as he had this woman? He slapped the ponies' flanks to make them run around the corral. He looked at his growing corn, and as he broke the little mud dam across his irrigation ditch, he felt the coolness of evening seep along his veins as the bright water spread through the narrow channels. Clay bluffs were not as fine as painted rock, there was too much adobe in this sand, but it was a fair place. The fire gleamed before his house, he heard the flow of water and the occasional stamp of a horse in the corral.

Slim Girl brought out the bottle and an orange.

'Do not make the drink, little sister, I do not want it. I think I shall try not taking it.'

She kept herself from looking at him. She was troubled.

'All right.'

145

What was this? Probably nothing. When one walks on the sheer edge of a precipice, the meaningless fall of a stone over the side momentarily stops the heart. She studied him while they ate. She began to talk with him gravely of the life they were to make together, of the happiness that was in store for them.

He said to himself, 'She was bothered when I refused that drink, the way she looked at me afterwards. She is nervous about me. I have done that, by acting as I have. Now she is trying to tell me how she really is; she is talking true; I know. I have wronged her.'

She saw the last trailing clouds pass from him. That evening was perfect, so perfect that, with his doubts banished and the feeling of intimacy upon him, he almost told her everything he had done and thought, but he postponed. It was the last of its kind for many days.

Like an ancient magician who, by saying the forbidden names, evoked genii whom he could not then drive back, Laughing Boy had given form to thoughts which were not to be forgotten. Unhappily for himself, he was no fool, and of an honest habit of thought. There was love in that place, and sometimes happiness, but if a religious-minded Navajo had entered there, he would have felt that the air was empty.

IV

Slim Girl continued weaving despite the poor sales, because she found relief and, one might say, a confidant in her craft. And then, they two, working side by side, reconstructed at least the outward signs of the harmony that was gone.

He eased his soul by shaping the half-stubborn, half-willing metal. It is a matter of patience, from the lump or the coins to the bar, from the bar to the bracelet. This, the most precious and beautiful of metals, is the easiest to work. That is a gift of the gods. Slow, slow, under successive light strokes the bar becomes longer, flatter, thinner: it is struck and it grows towards its appointed shape.

I am impatient these days, I get tired of the finishing. One must have one's mind made up to it from the start, from four Mexican coins to the finely finished ornament; one must see it as it will be, and not stop short of what he has seen.

Having woven about a foot of blanket, the head-sticks of the loom are lowered, and the finished part is rolled around the foot-sticks, out of sight.

This is like time. Here, this little part showing, where I am weaving, is the present; the past is rolled up and gone; there are those empty warp cords above me. The weft is like handling a nervous horse; I lead the blue strand gently to the green, or it will break; I hate to break a strand, the knot where it is mended will always show, a blemish. But then, I pound the fork and the batten down hard, hard; they lock the weave and that much more is past.

He was curving the strip of flattened silver. This bracelet is coming out just as I thought of it. One must know his design before he starts; when this strip was still four coins, I knew that there would be tracks pointing one way from each end to the centre, clouds at each end, and that stone where the tracks meet. How do I know it? Not all men can; what is it I have? The Mexicans are lazy, their money is pure, soft silver; the American coins have something in them to make them hard, they are hard to work with. Those Americans!

Her fingers were deft, and she pulled at the warp like a harp-player. I am not sure I like this pattern, but it is too late to change it. No, it is a good pattern. Should I unravel all I have done, when it grows so slowly? When the blanket has been started, it is too late to change. The man who is always coming back to where he started, to figure out another road, will never get far from home. I wish I could just think my design and have it woven at an American mill. No, I don't; it is because I toiled over them that I love them.

The turquoise is the important thing in this bracelet. I looked at it and saw the setting for it. But much of the time now I cannot think well, I am not myself. I have no design for myself, I do not know the nature of my jewel. I am hammering a piece of silver, and I cannot stop hammering, every day is another stroke; yet I do not know what it is to be. In the end it may be just a piece of good metal pounded flat. I do not know my design.

147

This blanket is like the other things. I am always being uncertain now. It is all like this blanket. Shall I unravel it, when I have been so long in getting so far? The design is set, a blanket with a broken design would be absurd, a failure. The only thing to do is to carry it through, with softness and with strength. My design is set.

CHAPTER SEVENTEEN

I

As summer drew to a close, Laughing Boy took to spending more time than was necessary with his horses. Sometimes he would crave company, and, if he found it, would be sociable and garrulous; at other times he kept very much to himself. No one who met him then for the first time would have named him 'Laughing Boy.' Locally he was known as 'Horse Trader,' and latterly one Indian had applied to him, in jest, the name of the legendary character 'Turns His Back,' which bade fair to stick. Partly he liked to be away from home because of the chance of a happy return. If she were waiting for him, if she had not been in to town, if he was tired from the long ride and at peace with himself, the old spell would surround them. If she was just back from that work of hers, or if she came in after he did, she overtired, brooding, and a little nervous, it was a failure. Once or twice they quarrelled; she had an amazingly sharp and clever tongue. The quarrels ended in reconciliation and passion which exhausted them both without bringing peace to either.

On one day, when autumn had begun to take the weight out of the noon sunshine, he sat basking on a hillock, smoking, with his pony beside him. He was lazily content, and comfortable enough within himself not to mind the sight of a human approaching. He felt like talking to some one.

The jogging dot drew nearer. Still looking black, the motion of the shoulders told that it was an Indian. Yes, and probably a Navajo, with a flaming scarlet headband. Laughing Boy sat up straight. He knew that bald-faced chestnut, he knew that swing of the whip hand. He made sure. He was surprised, curious, and delighted. What brought his friend so far from home? he rose to his feet. Jesting Squaw's Son slowed from lope to trot, to a walk, and stopped beside him.

'*Ei-yei*, my friend!' Laughing Boy took his hand. 'It is good to see you!'

'My friend.' He smiled, but he dismounted slowly, and his eyes were hurt. 'I am glad to find you.'

'Sit down. A cigarette?'

'Yes.'

'Where are you going?'

'Just riding around.'

'What is the news at T'o Tlakai?'

'All well. Your people are all well. Your sister, the one who married Bay Horse, has a son. The other one has just married Yellow Foot's Son.'

'Good.'

'There has been good rain, and the traders are paying twenty, twenty-five cents for wool.'

'Good.'

'And you, tell?'

'All well. Our goods sell well, the corn was fine this year. All well.'

They smoked.

'It is good to see you.'

Jesting Squaw's Son made no answer. Laughing Boy studied him; he was too quiet.

'What brings you so far from home?'

'Nothing, just riding around.'

'You will come to our hogahn?'

'Yes.'

They finished their cigarettes, and sat looking at nothing. There was a pleasant, afternoon feeling that tended to make talk slow, the smell of the warm sand,

149

quietness. After about five minues, Laughing Boy said:

'You might as well show me your true thought. It is all around you like a cloud. It is what you are thinking of all the time you are talking about anything else. You are hurt, What hurts you, whom I have called friend, hurts me.'

'You are right. Give me tobacco.'

He rolled another cigarette and smoked it through before he began to speak.

'You remember that joke we played on Narrow Nose at Gomulli T'o? Do you suppose we did anything bad by accident? Did we start any evil working?'

'What makes you think that?'

'You remember, I said I was bringing back a wife from Maito. That made me wonder. I went to Maito a little while ago.' He was looking at the tips of his fingers. Now he paused.

'We wanted to trade a cow for some sheep. Your brother and White Goat and I were riding along. We saw a Pah-Ute driving a cow he had taken from the Mormons, so we took it away from him. There is no pasture for cattle up there, but we heard of a man at Maito who kept a herd. So we took it down to him. His name is Alkali Water.

'The cow was pretty thin. We were there three nights trading on it.

'I saw his daughter. At the end of the first day I knew that I had been born only for her, that that was what I had always been waiting for. I was all one piece, everything in me was to one purpose. I do not know how to say it.'

'I know.'

'Yes, you know. That is why I am here. I know now why good men sometimes have to do with other people's wives. I have learned a great deal about myself.

'I shall not try to say what she looked like. What would be the use? She was not small, like your wife; she was strong. Her eyes and mouth were beautiful, she was beautiful, and you could see beauty inside her by her eyes and her mouth.

'We stayed there for three nights, for three nights and two days I was watching her and listening to her. I think she felt as I did; we did not speak to each other, hardly at all. When we went away she looked at me.

150

'I waited a few days at home. I was very happy; I did not know such happiness could exist. Then I returned to Maito. I wanted to see her again, to be sure, and to find out her clan before I asked my mother to ask for her. I did not want anyone to be able to object, as they might, since she did not live near us.

'I cannot make up songs as you do, but I made up a pretty good one. I sang all along the trail. I neared her hogahn galloping and singing the Wildcat Song. She was coming out along the trail towards me. I galloped close to her and reined up short, in a handsome way. She came beside my horse and laid her hand on its neck.

' "My friend," she said.

'I was so happy then that there is no name for it. There was no earth under me, I had no limits. Then she went on.

' "You must go away, you must not see me again. I must not see you," she said.

'I asked, "Why?"

'She said, "What is your clan?"

'I told her, "I am an Eshlini."

'She lowered her head, then she looked up again. Her face looked calm, but her eyes were wounded. "I, too, am an Eshlini," she said.

'We touched hands, and I rode away.'

Jesting Squaw's Son bowed his head on his knees. Laughing Boy felt his throat hurt, and yet in a curious way he felt better than he had in a long time. He was taken out of himself; he needed something like this.

'I could not go home then. I rode to T'o Atinda Haska Mesa, and went up to the top of it. I have been there a day and two nights. I did not eat. Why should I?

'At first I did not even think. I was just wild at first. All I could do was remember that happiness, that had been for nothing. I felt like asking her to come with me even so. I frightened myself. Am I an animal? Would I sleep with my sister? I did not know what to do. Why could she not have been a Tahtchini or a Lucau or an Eskhontsoni? But it was not her fault. And could I curse my mother because she was not a Bitahni or a T'o Dotsoni or a Nahkai?

151

'Then I got myself calmer. I could not have her. I made up my mind to it. I accepted it. But I still loved her. I still do. I still remember that happiness.

'That is very bad, it is beastly. My heart must be bad. I am frightened. Perhaps I should kill myself. Why not?

'I came here to see you. I did not want to go home to all my people. Perhaps you can help me. That is all.'

Laughing Boy stared into the ground. He was shocked, and his heart was wrung. He had never imagined that such a thing could happen; had it been told him of some unknown man, he would have supposed there was something bad about him to start with. It was such a disaster as an angry god might send, as though one heard in some legend, 'He went mad and fell in love with a woman of his own clan.' But his friend was good, all good. He knew what he was suffering. He remembered his feelings those first days at the dance. He thought hard. They must have sat for half an hour there before he spoke.

'Do not kill yourself. And do not feel ashamed, do not think you have sinned, or your heart is bad. No, you have shown it is good, I think. It would be bad if you kept on wanting to marry her, but what has happened to you is not something you do yourself. It is as though you were shot with an arrow.

'I nearly went away with my wife without asking her clan. We spoke directly to each other, without shame, when we saw there was nothing else to do.

'It is not your fault that you were shot. Suppose you had starved for a week, and some American, trying to be funny, the way they do, offered you fish to eat. If you ate it, it would be bad, but if your belly clamoured for it while you refused it, could you be blamed? No, you would have done a good thing, I think. You have done a good thing, a very hard thing. I think well of you.'

Jesting Squaw's Son gazed at him searchingly, and saw that he meant what he said.

'I think you are right. You have cured me of a deep wound. Thank you.'

'Let us start home. There are some of my horses in that little cañon, we shall get one, and turn yours

152

loose. It looks thin. There is pasture there, it will not wander.'

They caught fresh horses, and Jesting Squaw's Son exclaimed at the height of the grass, which in some places grew over a foot, in clumps. There was some like that at Dennihuitso, and in Kiet Siel Buckho, but not at this time of year.

They jog-trotted towards Chiziai, silent most of the time, talking occasionally.

'Up there, now, they do not call you by your old name,' Jesting Squaw's Son said, and hesitated. Even when he is a close friend, one is not free about discussing a man's name before him.

'I am not surprised.'

'They call you "Went Away." Your uncle calls you "Blind Eyes." '

'Unh! He would. Well, I am changed, it is right that my name should change.'

Jesting Squaw's Son trailed his rope to get the kinks out of it. Coiling it again, 'But they miss you. You will always be welcome.'

'In the end, we shall return.'

'You live close to the Iron Trail?'

'On the other side of it.'

'*Ei-yei!* A good place?'

'You will see, a fine place, but we cannot turn our horses out there, as it is Americans' country.'

'But you are near the Zuñis, too.'

'About a day's hard ride that way. I trade with them—horses for turquoise.'

'Have you any children?'

'Not now. We have a plan. We are making much money now, we are working as hard as we can. You would not believe how fast we make it. In a year or two we shall return to T'o Tlakai; we shall have perhaps fifty, perhaps sixty hundreds of dollars, in money and silver and horses, I think.'

'*Ei-yei!*'

'We shall be very rich. With that to start on, we shall be rich all our lives. We shall have our children then, we shall have a beautiful life. It is her idea, she thought of it. She takes care of the money, she trades with the Americans. She is remarkable.'

153

'You must be very happy.'
'I am.' He meant it.

II

Laughing Boy showed off the town, the irrigated strip, the railroad to his interested friend. Most delightfully, a passenger train went by; Jesting Squaw's Son sat his bolting, bucking horse with his head over his shoulder, his eyes glued on the marvel. His presence changed everything. Laughing Boy led him through the narrow place between the clay bluffs to his adobe house, the corral, the ditches and the hummocks of the summer's field, the sapling peaches. Jesting Squaw's Son admired, and a pain ran through him that there was not his own house and fields, and his own wife waiting by the fire.

Slim Girl came to the door. The autumn nights were already cold enough for the cooking to be done indoors. She greeted the visitor correctly, hospitably, and saw that her husband, although he seemed grave, was at peace with himself.

At the first moment when they were alone, Laughing Boy explained the situation, watching her anxiously. She nodded her head.

'Poor man, I am sorry for him. We must help him. He is going to get over his love, I think. He is already reconciled to it. It is that in combination with the other that worries him, I think.' Her husband, after a moment's thought, agreed. 'Now this is what we must do; talk about what will keep him interested, talk about things you have done together, talk of what will remind him of the good taste of life in his mouth. Do not try to make him laugh, do not try to comfort him. We shall show him new things. I shall give him some of your drink, I shall talk about the Americans. Now, I think, he is keeping one thing in his mind all the time, we must make him let go of it. Do you see?'

'Yes, that is very good.'

Truly, his wife was a remarkable woman, so wise, so right. Hearing his friend returning, he kissed her quickly.

That evening was blissful, so harmonious that in the middle of it Jesting Squaw's Son excused himself, went down to the corral, and cried into the shoulder of the first available horse. A horse, warm and silky is very nice to cry into when it stands still. The tears came readily. He had not cried before.

He stayed for three weeks, riding the range with Laughing Boy, watching the silversmithing, going down to see the trains pass by. He spent an entranced and delighted afternoon behind a bush, watching three negroes shoot craps, and nearly frightened them to death when he stood up suddenly, not five feet from them, bow in hand, to go away. He forgot about Alkali Water's daughter for hours at a time, until she became a curious, sad memory. He gave much thought to his hosts.

The novelty idea had been a good one, and they had plenty to offer, from the railroad and the cocktail, with its taste and surprising effect, to Slim Girl's talk of Americans. At night she spoke of their ways, of California, and of the other nations of people like Americans of whom she had heard, across Wide Water, toning down the more amazing things to credibility. They compared her knowledge with their experience on the reservation, and discussed the Americans' works, the good and bad things their coming had brought to the Navajo. They talked about the posse that hunted Blunt Nose, and stories of old times and the soldiers. That would lead to old wars with the Utes and the Jicarillas and the Stone House people, and they argued whether they gained or lost under the present enforced peace. Laughing Boy and Slim Girl enjoyed themselves enormously.

It was cold enough for a blanket over the shoulder, the day that Jesting Squaw's Son and Laughing Boy rode out to the pasture and caught his horse. Laughing Boy was sad at his friend's departure. They mounted their animals and clasped hands.

'I shall wait for you in the North.'

'We shall come, but I hope you will visit us here again.'

'I hope you will come too soon for that. I have lived in your house, I have seen you. You are both happy,

I think; you are both in love. But you are afraid. All the time you are enjoying yourselves you are watching for something over your shoulders, I think. I do not understand this. It is what I saw. This life of yours, it all looks like The People's life; only her going into town is strange. But it is not just she, it is you both that are not living like us, I think. I do not know what it is, but you are wearing moccasins that do not fit you. The sooner you both come back to your own people, the better, I think.

'I shall be waiting for you. You have restored my life.'

'It will be a good day when we meet again.'

It was a pity he was gone; he had been such pleasant company. They had been too much alone, and he had cured that. He had misunderstood it, too. He wanted to see his wife and talk about their guest. He hurried home.

CHAPTER EIGHTEEN

I

IT had come round to the beginning of Little Snow Moon again, a time of year when horses, seeking feed, are likely to wander. Laughing Boy kept close watch on his herd, and was little surprised, on one day of high wind that covered the tracks, to find a stallion, a three-year-old, missing. It must have been gone for some time; he was unable to find it in the immediate district, and soon lost its trail completely. Returning to his house, he made preparations to be away for a week in search of it; the animal was valuable.

Slim Girl procured chocolate and other dainties for

him. The weather was no longer warm, he could not tell where he might camp, she felt that he would undergo hardships. But, as he said, one could not let as good a pony as that wander at will in a country entirely populated by connoisseurs and lovers of horse-flesh.

Four days passed in vain. On the fifth, acting on the tip of a Hopi mail carrier, he picked up its trail north of Winslow. The next morning he found it, scarcely fifteen miles from Los Palos.

It had no mind to go back to the herd. At first sight of him it began walking as it grazed, then, seeing him draw slightly nearer, broke into a trot, and thus all morning, matching its pace to his, kept a quarter of a mile between them. He tried to edge it towards the left, but it seemed to guess his intention, taking advantage of a butte that prevented heading off to break sharply right and gallop furiously a mile in the direction of the railroad. It was never panicked, never too hurried, expending always just enough effort.

As he pursued, Laughing Boy admired. The chestnut stallion was coming into its strength, gleaming, round quarters, bunched muscles at the juncture of the throat and chest, a ripple of highlight and shadow on the withers, arched neck, pricked small Arab ears, bony head, eyes and nostrils of character and intelligence. It was one of those ponies, occasionally to be found, in which one reads a page of the history of that country; a throwback to Spanish *Conquistadores* and dainty-hooved, bony-faced horses from Arabia.

Midday was warm, sandy dust rose from the trail in clouds. Laughing Boy munched raisins and chocolate as he rode, remembering when the men on the posse had offered him the same rations. That girl, she was a whole war-party in herself! The stallion balked at the railroad tracks, considered, and cleared them with a nervous leap.

Now Laughing Boy thought he had it; the dingy suburbs of the town, on the far side from his hogahn, made a half-circle before them. He advanced cautiously. It was a question of getting it cornered so that he could dismount, for Navajos do not rope from the saddle. Now the stallion began to rush, and the work

157

became fast—a break to the right, Laughing Boy, pouring leather into his pony, headed it, then left, and the houses turned it again. A desperate race to prevent a desperate attempt to break back across the tracks; it wheeled again, straight between two houses, stallion and mounted man going like fury, to the admiration of an old Mexican woman and the clamorous terror of a sleeping cur.

The stallion drew away from him, and he slowed his pace. It cantered past an adobe house standing alone under two cottonwoods, and, just beyond, fell to grazing in a little hollow. Laughing Boy advanced cautiously, using the house as cover. He figured that he could dismount behind it, and with a quick rush corner the animal in the angle of two wire fences protecting irrigated fields. The pony was already moving into the trap, unconscious of the wire.

He rode at a walk, close along the mud wall from which the sun was reflected with a stuffy, muddy smell. As he passed the window, he looked in, and reined his horse so suddenly that it reared, while his heart stopped for a moment and his whole body was a great choking. An agonized, clear voice cried out, inside,

'Sha hast'ien, sha hast'ien codji!—My husband, my husband there!' And a man said, 'My God!'

Before he had started thinking, he wheeled and rode madly for the door side. As he came around the corner, an American, hatless, came out, saw man and horse coming upon him, jumped aside and stood for a moment. His hands strung his bow without conscious willing. The man began to run towards the town. Arrow leaped to string almost of itself, hands and arms functioned, drew, released, but the excited pony would not keep still and the missile went wide, to the right. A second was in the air before the first landed, but it passed just over the man's shoulder, hard by the ear, startling him into an amazing leap and burst of speed. There was something ridiculous about it which calmed Laughing Boy. He steadied his pony and shot with care. The arrow struck just below the shoulder, the American fell doubled up, almost turning a somersault, picked himself up, and with a last effort rounded the corner between the outermost houses at the end of the straggling street.

Calmly, he waited before the house. Afterwards there were going to be terrible feelings and thoughts, but now he knew what was to be done. His face showed no particular age, young or old; it was hardly the face of an individual, rather, of a race.

Slim Girl stood in the doorway, neat, dressed in American clothes.

'Come here, little sister.' Voice even and impersonal.

She walked slowly. For the first time since he had known her, he saw that her self-possession was only a surface. She looked as though a searing light were shining before her, showing her Hell. She stood beside his saddle.

'Did you kill him?'

'No, I hit him in the shoulder.'

This was the fourth arrow. It was right that such a thing should happen by fours. The gods were in it.

'You have killed us both, I think.'

She did not answer. He looked at her eyes, then avoided them; not from shame, but because there was too much in them. He did not want to begin to realize yet. He must keep his head. He thought how beautiful she was, and began to feel the greatness of his loss.

'You understand what I am doing?'

Again she did not answer.

He notched the fourth arrow meticulously, drew to the head, released. The twang of the string echoed and reached over great spaces. At the sound, he became aware of agony pent up behind his mind like high waters behind a too-slight dam, about to break through and carry away. At the same time, with the instant of releasing the string, he saw her open right hand pass across the face of the bow, her left arm rise. Now she stood, smiling stiffly, her eyes her own again. Her right hand was still in front of the bow in a stiff, quaint gesture. There was blood on the tips of the fingers. The arrow stood, through nearly to the feathers, in her left forearm.

He saw her as at a great distance. This was all wrong, something impossible had happened. She held her arm up rigidly, her lips remained set in that stiff

159

smile. In a moment she was going to speak. The feelings and realizations were coming upon him. He lifted the reins and rode slowly around the corner of the house.

The stallion watched him nervously.

'Go your way, little brother.' He watched the animal as he rode past, then he contemplated the ears of his mount. 'You are saddled and ridden, but you are better off than I. This would be a good world if we were all geldings, I think.'

II

The pony, wandering unguided, brought him slowly within sight of his house. He turned it aside, making a wide circle to come to the high place by the tree from the other side. The house, the field of corn-stubble, the five struggling peach trees, the corral, all very dear, stood like unanswerable refutations in the long streaks of afternoon shadow. As the sight of the perfect, familiar body of some one just dead, or the little possessions, the objects just set down, ready to be picked up again as always, again and again render that death incredible, so was the sight of these things to Laughing Boy. Her loom stood under the brush sun-shelter before the door, with a half-finished blanket rolled at its foot. Unbelievable, not true, only—it was so. He went through the past day, searched the farther past, as though by travelling it again he could find where the false trail branched off, and reduce this calamity to an error.

Ten thousand things told him that what he had learned was ridiculous, but it always led again to the window in the adobe house and the clear frightened voice crying, '*Sha hast'ien, sha hast'ien codji!*'

Now it was time to think, but an hour or more passed before he could prevent the beginnings of thought from turning to frantic revolt. Prayer helped him. He got himself in hand and rolled a cigarette.

Now I must choose between her and myself. If I stay with her, I lose myself, really. I am a man. I am a warrior. If I do not give her up, I become some-thing else from what I have always been. The world

160

changes, the good things, the bad things, all change for me. And they change for the bad. I cannot shoot her again. I cannot do that thing. If I leave her, I am still I, but I and the world are dead. Oh, my friend, my friend, your choice was so simple, you were lucky. The arrow only grazed you; it has gone through my bowels. And when it came my turn to send the arrow back, I missed.

Oh, well named, Came With War, Came With War, oh, beautiful! Why do they give women names about war? I know all about that now. My uncle was right. I cannot go now and see their faces. Kill myself. That would settle it. But not now, not in this place. If it keeps on being like this, I shall do that, in my own country. Came With War, Came With War, Slim Girl, you coyote, you devil, you bad woman.

I must go away. I cannot stay with her. She is worth everything in the world, but there is something in me that I have no right to trade for her. That is what I must do.

He struggled for a long time, facing this decision, until it sank into him. The sun was low, the little valley between the buttes was all shadow. He had not seen her return, and hoped she had not. There would be begging, talk, tears—terrible. If she were not there, he would just take his things and go; the missing goods would explain.

It was all too much for him. He felt as if he were shaken by high winds. That little house down there was a place of waiting torment. He stood, clutching his hands together and weaving his head from side to side. This was far worse than war. He turned to the gods, making the prayer of a man going alone to battle:

'Shinahashé nageï, nageï, alili kat' bitashah . . .
'I am thinking about the enemy gods, the enemy gods, among their weapons now I wander.
    A-yé-yé-yé-ya-hai!
Now Slayer of Enemy Gods, I go down alone among them,
    The enemy gods, the enemy gods, I wander among their weapons.

161

Touched with the tops of the mountains, I go down alone
     among them,
  The enemy gods, the enemy gods, I wander among their
     weapons.
Now on the old age trail, now on the path of beauty
     walking,
  The enemy gods, the enemy gods, I wander among their
     weapons.'

It was apposite, and it helped enormously. Now it
was not merely he battling with these terrific things,
now the unseen power of good would uphold him.
Leading his horse, he went down slowly to his house.

CHAPTER NINETEEN

I

THERE were her tracks, wind-blurred in the sand.
She must have come straight home, arriving before
he reached the high place. With dread he entered
the door, grateful for the half-darkness inside. She
had got back into Navajo clothes, moccasins, skirt,
and sash, but her blouse was only pulled over the
right shoulder, leaving the left arm and breast bare.
Did she think—? He saw her as an enemy.

'I am going away.'

'All right. But first pull this out; I am not strong
enough.' She held out her arm with the arrow through
it.

He stared at it, and it made him feel sick. He was
frankly avoiding her face, but he knew that the blood
was gone from beneath the bronze surface, leaving it
yellow-white with a green tinge under it. He kept on
looking at the arrow, his arrow, with his marks on it.

'You must come out to the light.'

She rose with difficulty, steadying herself against the wall. He supported her to the door.

The arrow had passed through the flesh of the under side of her arm, just missing the artery and the bone. The shaft stood out on both sides. From the barbed, iron head to the wound there was blood in the zigzag lightning grooves. The roundness of her arm was caked with dried blood and already somewhat swollen. To the one side was the barbed point, to the other were the eagle feathers and the wrappings. He took out his knife.

'I shall try not to make it wiggle,' he said.

'What are you going to do?'

'Cut it off just by the hole; I can't pull all that through your arm.'

'It is a good arrow. Pull it through.'

There was never another woman like this one. 'Do you think I would use this again?'

He held her arm very carefully, he cut with all possible gentleness, but the shaft moved and moved again. He heard her take in her breath and looked quickly to see her teeth clenched on her lower lip. She should have been a man. Every dart of pain in her arm went doubly through his heart. The wood was cut short, just above the wound.

'Now,' he said, 'are you ready?'

'Pull.'

He jerked it out. She had not moved. She was rigid and her eyes were almost glassy, but she had not made a sign. He still knelt, staring at her, at the fresh blood welling, and at the red stump of the arrow in his hand. She was brave, brave.

She whispered, 'Get me some of the whiskey.'

He gave her a stiff dose in a cup. She emptied it at once, and sighed. A little colour came back.

'It will be dark soon. You had better go now. I can take care of myself. But before you go, know this: whatever you have seen, I love you and you only and altogether. Good-bye.'

She handed him back the cup. As he took it, their fingers touched, and he looked into her eyes. Something snapped inside of him. He fell forward, his head close to his knees, and began sobbing. She laid her hand on his shoulder.

'You have been hasty, I think. One should not turn up a new trail without looking around. And you have not eaten, you are tired. This has been hard for you. In a minute I shall heat some coffee, and we can talk straight about this.'

II

The night was plenty sharp enough for a fire indoors. Under her directions he prepared canned goods and coffee, but neither of them did more than toy with the food. He had a feeling that she was going to find a solution for them; the experience that they had just shared had changed everything again, he didn't know where he was. Landmarks shifted too quickly, he was in a turmoil once more, with his determinations to be made anew.

She asked him to roll her a cigarette; then,

'Make the drink as you have seen me do, only make some for me, too.'

He hesitated.

'Do not be afraid of my medicine.'

He muttered a denial and fixed the drink. She sipped at hers slowly. She needed strength, for she was nearly exhausted, and there was a battle to be fought.

'You cannot know whether a thing is good or bad unless you know all about it, and the cause of it. I do not try to say that what I have done is good, but I want to tell you my story, that you do not know; then you can judge rightly.'

He hardly had expected her to come so directly to the point. He prepared to sift lies.

'Roll me a cigarette.

'I have to begin way back. Hear me.

'When I was still a little girl, they took me away to the all-year school at Wide Water, as you know. They took me because I did well at the day school at Zhil Tséchiel, so they wanted me to learn more. I told you how they tried to make us not be Indians; they succeeded pretty well. I wanted to be American.

I forgot the gods then, I followed the Jesus trail. I did well, then, at that school.

'While I was there both my father and mother went underground. My mother had no brothers or sisters living, and I was her only child. I saw no reason for returning to The People. I was an American, with an American name, thinking in American.

'I grew up. I wanted to work for Washindon on a reservation, like that Papago woman who writes papers for the American Chief at T'o Nanasdési. But I could not get that work right away, so they said I could work for a preacher at Kien Doghaiyoi—you know that big town? The Americans call it Oñate.'

'I have heard.' He was studying her intently. Her voice came low and toneless; she spoke slowly, but behind it was something intense.

'I went there, about three years ago. I loved the Jesus trail; I thought it was very good to work for a preacher. That way it was.'

She stared into the fire as she took a sip of liquor.

'He was a good man, and his wife was very good. He did not let her have much to say. I worked pretty hard, but it was all right.

'I learned some strange things. I learned about the bad women—they make their living by lying down with men, just any men who will pay them. Some of them were Americans, some had been schoolgirls like me. The preacher used to preach against them sometimes; I thought, he did not need to do that. Something had happened to their faces, their eyes; their mouths were terrible. They were like something in a bad dream. That way I thought.

'Then by and by I fell in love with a man. He was big and good-looking and he talked pious. He was a cow-puncher; he worked on a ranch near there. Lots of American girls liked him. When he paid attention to me, I was flattered. He was wonderful, I thought. We should be married and have a ranch together; it was almost too good to believe, I thought.

'I was frightened when he wanted me to lie with him, but he made me feel all right. He knew all about how to make women forget themselves, that man.

'Then I saw I was going to have a child. The next

165

time he came to town, I asked him to marry me quickly. He made promises. Then he didn't come to town again, so I went to the ranch where he worked. He was angry when he saw me there. He offered me money, but I said I wanted marriage.

'I became frightened, I begged and I cried. He got very angry, he called me names. He said to get out of his way, he couldn't be bothered with a "squaw." That is a word Americans use to mean Indian women; it is contemptuous. I learned a lot then; right then I was not so young as I had been, I think.

'I went back to the preacher's. I was not afraid to tell him, but I was ashamed. I could not be calm about it, it was hard to say. I just walked in on them and said:

' "I am going to have a child. It is that man's. He will not marry me."

'They were astonished; then the preacher looked angry. He called me bad. He asked what good all my training had done me; he called me ungrateful. He said a lot of things. If I had waited until he got through, his wife would have spoken, and they would have taken care of me, I think. But I was finding out that every one said one thing and did another. The Jesus trail seemed to be a lie, too. I told him that. I threw his religion at him. Then he said all sorts of things about me, and ordered me out of his house.

'My money was soon gone. I went hungry. I thought I had shame written all over my face. But even then I was strong; I thought that the world had beaten me now, but I would keep on fighting and by and by I would beat it. But just then I was desperate.

'Then those bad women spoke to me. They took me in and fed me; they were kind, those bad women. All my ideas were turned upside down now. I did not care. My heart was numb. I learned their trade. I did what they did. In a few months so, with the baby in me, that made me very sick. They took care of me, those bad women.

'I suffered much pain, the child was born much too soon, dead. I was glad.

'When I was well, I went back to work among them. I had thought a lot, I learned a great deal. I saw how this new life was bad. I saw the faces, the empty hearts of those women, kind though they were. I hated all Americans, and I made up my mind that an American should pay for what an American had done. I remembered my true name. I would have gone to my people, but I did not know how, and I wanted to be paid back. I had my plan.

'I noticed one thing—that the men, when they went with those women, liked to be helped to fool themselves that they were with another kind of woman, that they were loved. I did not look like those women yet. I looked young, and decent. They liked that, those men. By then it meant nothing to me; it was just as if I cooked them a meal. It had nothing to do with love, nothing to do with what you know.

'I watched for my chance, and by and by I saw it—a man from the East, that one. He had good manners. He was lonely. And he did not have the poor ideas about Indians that most of these people have, that man.

'I was very careful with him. I did not do any of the things those women usually do to get money away from a man and be rid of him quickly. I acted as innocent as I knew how. He said he was sorry to see me leading such a life. I caught him. He was in Kien Doghaiyoi three nights, and all three nights he came to me. I found out all about him.

'Two weeks later he came back, and I saw him again. I had him, I thought.

'Ten days after that I came here to Chiziai. I had money. I took that house where you saw me. I watched and waited. He lives a day from there. On the fifth day he came in. I managed to meet him when he was alone. He was surprised and glad. I asked him to come to my house in the evening. I had food and much whiskey for him, so that finally he went to sleep.

'When he woke up in the morning, that was the test. He felt badly then, and ashamed to wake up in the house of a bad woman. I handed him his money, two hundred dollars, and told him to count it, that it was all there. Then I gave him coffee, and a little whiskey, and then food. He asked how much I wanted. I said I was not doing this for money. Then

I gave him a little more whiskey, and so I kept him all day. I did not let him get drunk, and I acted like a good woman who called him friend.

'The next morning he said he had to get back to work. He said he would see me when he came back to town, and he wished I was not what I was. He was lonely, that man. These were not his people, these Americans here they did not talk the same. Like a Navajo living among Apaches.'

Her voice was taking on a timbre of triumph.

'I said, "You will not find me here."'

'He said, "At Kien Doghaiyoi, then."'

'"No," I said, "I am through with all that. I only did it because I had to. I hated it."'

'He asked how that happened. I told him about half the truth and half lies, to make it sound better, saying I had been bad only a few weeks. Now I said an old Navajo whom I had always known was come for me; I did not love him, but he was a good man, and I was going to marry him. But first I wanted to see him—the American—I said, because he had been kind to me, because he was not like the others. So I had come here for just a few days, I said.

'He thought a little while. He said, "Stay." He said he would give me money. I pretended not to want to take money from him; I made him persuade me. I was afraid he might ask me to marry him, but he was not that much of a fool. Finally I said, "All right."

'I had conquered.'

There was a strong triumph in her voice at that last phrase; now it returned to the level, slow, tired speech.

'I told him I could not just live there, a Navajo woman. It would make talk, men would annoy me. It would be better if I married the old Navajo and lived near by, then I could meet him when he came to town. With whiskey, I said, that man could be kept happy. I said he was old.

'He did not want it to be known he was providing for a Navajo woman, so he agreed. He gave me fifty dollars.

'There was no Navajo.'

168

She paused. 'Roll me a cigarette.' She smoked it through, then resumed:

'I was not happy. I was provided for, I was revenging myself through him, but I was not living. I wanted my own people. I was all alone. That was why I made friends with Red Man. He is not good, that man. He did not care if I were bad, he hoped I might be bad with him. I never was, but I kept him hoping. With him I remembered the ways of The People, I became quick again in their speech. He helped me much. He is not all bad, that man.

'The People looked at me askance. I was a young woman living alone, they did not know how, so they made it up. They do that. Your uncle knows that talk. This went on for over a year. Then I saw you, and everything changed. I had thought I was dead to men, and now I knew I loved you. With you I could live, without you I was already dead.

'I was right. Our way of life, to which you have led me, my weaving, our songs, everything, is better than the Americans'. You have made this.

'I had enough, but I thought I could have better. I wanted it for you; you were giving back to me what the Americans had robbed from me since they took me from my mother's hogahn. I thought it right that an American should pay tribute to you and me, I thought it was the perfection of my revenge. After what had happened to me, things did not seem bad that seem bad to other people. So I kept on. I did not tell you, I knew you would not like it.

'I thought it was all right. What I did with him had nothing to do with what I did with you, it was just work. It was for us, for our life.

'And I did not want to herd sheep and grow heavy and ugly early from work, as Navajo women do. I wanted much money, and then to go North and have children with you and stay beautiful until I am old, as American women do. I was foolish.

'Then I saw your face in the window, and the world turned to ashes, and I knew that there were things that were worse than death. That is all, that is the truth. I have spoken.'

She sank back, exhausted, with closed eyes. Laughing Boy lit a cigarette from the fire. Then he said:

'I hear you. Sleep. It is well.' He squatted in the doorway, smoking.

III

He was at peace within himself. Now at last he knew his wife, now at last he understood her, and it was all right. Error not evil. Something inimical and proud in her had been destroyed. He was tired, emotionally drained, but he could let his smoke curl up to the stars and feel the cold air penetrate his blanket, calmly, while he thought and knew his own mind. He had a feeling, without any specific reason, that he should keep a vigil over Slim Girl, but he became so sleepy. He went in by the fire, pulled sheepskins about himself, and slept.

In the morning he brought her food and tended her wound. After they had eaten and smoked, he spoke.

'You have lived in a terrible world that I do not know. I cannot judge you by my world. I think I understand. You have deceived me, but you have not been untrue to me, I think. Life without you would be a kind of death. Now I know that I do not have to do what I thought I had to, and I am glad for it. Now I know you, and there is no more of this secret thing that has been a river between us.

'As soon as you are able, we shall go North. If there is a place where you have relatives, we can go there. If not, we can go to T'o Tlakai, or some place where your clan is strong, or wherever you wish. We shall get the sheep that my mother is keeping for me, and we shall buy others, and we shall live among The People. That is the only way, I think.

'Understand, if we go on together, it is in my world, The People's world, and not this world of Americans who have lost their way.'

They kissed.

'I shall be happy with you anywhere that you wish to take me. As you have said, there is nothing between us now. You have made up to me, and revenged me, for everything the Americans have done to me, My Slayer of Enemy Gods.'

'You must not call me that; it is wicked to call a human being by such a name.'

She answered him with another kiss. He thought he had never seen her look so happy. For the first time since he had known her, she looked as young as she was, a year or so younger than himself. Her face was full of peace.

They fell to planning. Reckoning their resources, they concluded that they had amassed the astounding sum of three thousand dollars in money, goods, and horses. He did not want to take what came through her lover, but she said:

'No; I took it like spoils in war. It was war I made with him. And you made it yours when your arrow struck him. And we both paid for it, I think.'

'Perhaps when he gets well he will send policemen after us.'

'No, I know him. He will say nothing; he will be ashamed, I think.'

CHAPTER TWENTY

I

DURING the interval, Laughing Boy moved most of his horses a couple of days' ride farther north, not far from Zhil Clichigi, where he penned them in a box cañon in which there was a spring and still a little feed. He bought provisions at a trading post on the road to T'o Hatchi. Slim Girl had confessed to him that the story about the warrant out for him on account of the Pah-Ute had been a lie, but, all things considered, she felt it best that he stay away from town. He said that it had seemed a little odd that there should be so much trouble over a Pah-Ute.

'No,' she said, 'they do not want any shooting.'

'That is true. Whenever there is cause for a fight, they want to send men to do the fighting, and only let us come as guides, like that time with Blunt Nose. They must be very fond of fighting, I think, and they have not enough of their own, so they do other people's fighting for them. It is a good thing and a bad thing.

'I do not understand them, those people. They stop us from raiding the Stone House People and the Mexicans, which is a pity; but they stop the Utes and the Comanches from raiding us. They brought in money and silver, and these goods for our clothes. They bring up water out of the ground for us. We are better off than before they came.

'But yet it does not matter whether they do good things or bad things or stupid things, I think. When one or two come among us, they are not bad. If they are, sometimes we kill them, as we did Yellow Beard at Kien Dotklish. But a lot of them and we cannot live together, I think. They do good things, and then they do something like taking a child away to school for five years. Around Lukachukai there are many men who went to school; they wear their hair short; they all hate Americans. I understand that now. There is no reason in what they do, they are blind, but in the end they will destroy everything that is different from them, or else what is different must destroy them. If you destroyed everything in me that is different from them, there would only be a quarter of a man left, I think. Look at what they tried to do to you. And yet they were not deliberately trying.

'Well, soon we shall be where there are few Americans, very few. And we shall see that our children never go to school.'

'Soon we shall be where there are very Americans'; that thought was constant in his mind. He was very happy, it was like a second honeymoon. He had kept all the good things of life, and he had saved himself. He saw that his wife depended on him; she was very tender and rather grave. He under-

stood her gravity, in view of her wound and all that
had happened. Soon in new surroundings there would
be cause for only happiness. A little readjustment,
a little helping her into a less comfortable life, but
her courage would make nothing of that.

She was very tender and very grave, and she was
thinking a great deal. That crisis like a blast of white
light had shown her life and herself, it had ended
her old independence. She had unravelled her blanket
back to the beginning, and started again with a design
which could not be woven without Laughing Boy, and
she knew that there could be no other design.

It would not be easy at first to be competent and
satisfactory up there; to make herself accepted and
liked, to do the dull things, to watch sheep and make
her own bread. But she would, and she could. They
would go to Oljeto, Moonlight Water, a pretty name
and a pretty place, if a childhood memory were true.
She had relatives there, and it was far from the long
arm of the American—wild country, with the un-
explored fastnesses towards Tsé Nanaazh and the
Pah-Utes. That would be better than dealing with his
relatives at T'o Tlakai, and it was near enough for
visiting.

'And we shall see that our children never go to
school.' She echoed that, and she longed for them—his
children. But the thought gave her pause. Now that
she was thinking as true as she knew how, for her
salvation, she wondered if she still could have a child.
She was young, but she had been through a lot. After
that one terrible time, instructed by the prostitutes
of Oñate, she had never put herself in danger of it—or
had she? She cast back carefully in her mind; she was
not sure. It was possible that she could, possible that
she could not. The thing stared her in the face like
a risen corpse.

Then what could she do? Have him take another
wife, who would bear them to him. Then in the end
he would love that other. He would not, of himself,
ever want her to go away, but that other would scheme
against her, the mother of his children. What would
there be in the world for her, a barren Indian, having

lost Laughing Boy? An unlocked door in a street by the railroad track, or death. Only death.

There must be children. After all, she was only frightening herself with a chance. When she was quite well, and rested, in their new home, she would put it to the test, and it would come out all right. So she was grave and very tender.

II

When her arm was almost well, Laughing Boy brought three of his best horses to the corral. They prepared to move in beautiful, clear, cold, sunny weather following a first light snow, the slight thawing of which assured them of water. Their goods made little bulk—well over a thousand dollars in silver, turquoise, and coral, several hundred dollars in coin, his jeweller's kit, her spindle, batten, cards, and fork, half a dozen choice blankets, some pots and pans and provisions. They carried a good deal on their saddles, and packed the rest, Navajo-fashion, which is to say badly, on the spare pony. They set out with fine blankets over their shoulders, their mounts prancing in the cold, their saddles and bridles heavy with silver and brass, leading the pack-horse by a multi-coloured horsehair rope, a splendid couple.

After a period of worrying, she had reacted, partly by deliberately living each day for itself only, partly by a natural and reasonable swing to optimism. So they were both gay as they rode, and chattered together of the future. Oljeto had been agreed upon for their new home. It was a good winter camp, he said, and he thought that at Segi Hatsosi or Adudjejiai, little over a day's ride distant, he could find an unclaimed fertile strip for summer. There is good water there, even in dry summers.

'You have seen the stone granaries we build,' he said. 'The rock around that part breaks easily into squares, there is lots of good adobe. I can build you a house as good as the one we just left. We shall make a tunnel like that for the smoke from the fire, and we shall have one of those wooden doors that swing. There will be no house like it around there, except the trader's at T'o Dnesji.'

She smiled. 'And a window?'

'Yes, but we cannot have that clear stone in it. We shall put a membrane across it, that will let in light, I think, but you cannot see through it.'

'That will be good enough.'

They came into the mouth of Chizbitsé Cañon. Here and there were fragments of petrified trees, all colours, some dull, some reflecting like marble, the many shades made brilliant by the thin blanket of snow around them, and the clear sunlight.

'*Ei-yei!* It is a place of jewels!'

They slowed from a jog-trot to a walk, looking about them at the reproductions of trunks, rings, branches, exact even to the way the snow lay upon them, beautiful in colour, and somehow frightfully dead.

'There is a piece I could use.' Laughing Boy dismounted and picked it up, marbled in ruddy blue and yellow. 'I can cut it up and polish it, and use it in rings and bow-guards.'

'Yes, it will be a new thing, if it is not too hard to work.'

They searched for a few minutes for more good fragments, then he mounted, shouted the packhorse back onto the trail, and they rode on.

III

Red Man, on his way to trade at Jadito, rode past the mouth of Chizbitsé. He had not breakfasted, but the clear weather, the liveliness of his new horse, kept him cheerful. He looked up the cañon, saw them, and thought,

'Those two!'

He crossed the cañon-mouth and stopped where a rock hid all but his head and shoulders. He was swept by an emotion of many factors which time and much mulling over had compounded into one.

I helped that woman, I took care of her. I ran her errands, I made life possible for her. I loved her, in a way. I knew she was bad with Americans, but she would never do it with me. I deserved it from her.

She made a fool of me instead. Why not me, too? Always putting me off and getting around me. And then that fool came out of nowhere and she gave him everything. Him! And he threatened me. *He* told *me* what to do.

All this through many months had become a single feeling. They were riding slowly, leaning towards each other, talking. Faintly, he heard her laugh. There was a pack-animal in front of them—they were going on a visit somewhere, very rich, with a pack-horse.

He thought, 'There goes the man who may send an arrow into me some day.' It made the small of his back squirm.

He took up his rifle, aimed high for distance, and fired. The gun had not been cleaned for several weeks, his hands were cold, and the pony moved. He fired three times, then ducked low behind the rock, and began riding.

Laughing Boy heard the shots, turned, and ducked as two bullets snapped close to him, before he saw Slim Girl slump forward in the saddle. He threw his arm about her, caught her rein, and drove the horses to a gallop. The pack-animal, startled by the rush behind him, raced ahead. When you have only a bow, and an unseen person or persons begins shooting liberally with a rifle. it is no time for gestures of valour or revenge.

They rode thus for about a mile, and then, still seeing no one behind them, drew rein. Here the cañon was wide, and on one side a cleft led into Chizbitsé Mesa, up a slow incline. In there he turned, until at the end of the box cañon sheer cliffs stopped them.

Slim Girl was silent and quite limp as he lowered her from her saddle and placed her on a couch of blankets. Once at ease there, she moaned and asked for water. Her eyes were narrowed and her lips drawn slightly back. He made a fire and melted snow, she drank eagerly.

The bullet had gone clean through her; she was soaked with blood. He did what he could to staunch the flow, and arranged her as comfortably as possible. Occasionally she moaned, then said quite clearly:

'No. I will be brave. Give me a cigarette, and raise my head a little.'

She had scarcely strength to smoke, and she began to cough.

'This is the end, my husband, my beloved.' Her voice was faint, and she paused after every few words. 'Do not try to avenge me. Promise me that.'

'I promise.' He knelt facing her, unmoving, with lines in his face like carving.

'I think this was meant to happen. Perhaps it is right, I think. After all that had happened to me, perhaps I could not have had children. The Americans spoiled me for a Navajo life, but I shall die a Navajo, now.' She spoke very slowly, with long waits while she lay with closed eyes and her hands clenched. 'I have saved my soul through you. I have been very happy with you. This last little while, I found myself, I found truth with you.' She broke into coughing, and then was silent for almost five minutes.

'I say all this so you shall know that it has not been in vain. You will go on and live and remember me, you have changed because of me; in you I shall live.

'I have come home. I shall die at home, I shall be buried like my People. It is *hozoji*.'

He had no words at all.

'I love you so much. Kiss me.'

He bent over her, her arm clutched about his neck, he lifted her shoulders against his chest. Her eyes were closed and she kissed him with cool, closed lips of love, not of passion.

She opened her eyes, drew back her head, and smiled at him. Then she said in a clear voice,

'Nayeinezgani!—Slayer of Enemy Gods.'

And so speaking, smiling, died.

Then she is dead. Then it is all over. But just a little while ago we were laughing together and picking up stones. We were so happy together. Now it is all over. But we had everything arranged, we were going North, we had all our goods, our silver, our blankets. I was going to make her a ring with that purple stone. I was going to build her a house. Now it is all over. There is no sense in it. *Ei-ee*, Divine Ones! *Ei*, Slim Girl, Came With War!

He threw himself upon her body and pressed his mouth to hers. Her lips were cold, she was cold and inert all over. It was inhuman, it was dead. He drew back and rose to his feet with a revulsion of fear, then grew calm.

This is not she, not Slim Girl, Brave Alone, not Came With War, not my wife. This is something she left behind. It is dead, it never had life; it was she inside it who gave it life. I am not afraid of it, and can I ever be afraid of you, oh, beautiful? I shall be calm, I shall bury it, a Navajo burial.

He knelt beside her body and began to sob. After a while he thought, she would not like me to do this. I must bury her before it gets dark. It will snow soon. All alone I went with her, alone I lived with her and knew her beauty, now I alone shall bury her. She was not meant for common knowledge, she was not part of ordinary life, that many people should partake of her.

IV

The pack-horse had disappeared, but before going it had, like a wise animal, rolled its pack off. He collected all their goods and divided them into two equal parts. Most of the time he was not really thinking, but dully following out with slow movements what seemed to be a foreordained course. It occurred to him that the riches that came through the American ought to be thrown away, but he remembered what she had said about that. In jewelry and blankets it had been transmuted. He picked up one of the heaps of coin. That was a lot of money. They had suffered a lot for it, she had suffered so much. He set it down again.

The farthest corner of the cliffs made a niche about twelve feet square, in which the rocks came to the ground sheer, or slightly overhanging, without talus. Here he carried her, and set her in the farthest recess. He walked carefully, avoiding bushes, observing all the requirements, in so far as was possible for a single individual. Over her he put her blankets, at her head, food, by her hands, her weaving tools, cooking implements at her feet. He covered her form with silver and turquoise and coral and coins. As he arranged her, he prayed. Then he looked about for fair-sized slabs, of which there were plenty round about, in the talus. He began to bring them, covering her. He had placed the first few, at her feet, when he straightened up and stood still. He walked to his own pile of goods and looked at it. Returning to her, he found her arm under the blankets, and took from it a thin, gold bracelet that she had bought in California. From his own goods he set aside the finest saddle-blanket of her weaving, an old trade blanket, a coffee-pot and coffee. Bundling all the rest together, he carried it to the grave and spread it over her. Slowly he took off his heavy silver belt, his turquoise and coral necklace, his two bracelets, his garnet ring and his turquoise ring, his earrings of turquoise matrix, laying each one gently upon the heap. He changed his old bow-guard for one he had made at their house. Remembering something, he went to his pony, took off his silver-mounted bridle, and added it. With difficulty, he forced the thin gold circle up over his right hand, taking some of his skin with it: it was but little wider than his wrist, it would not come off easily. Then he continued covering her. It began to snow, in large, soft, slow flakes out of a grey-white sky.

It was nearly dark when he had laid on the last stone, and he began to be aware that he was weary. Blowing cigarette smoke four ways, he stood in prayer for a minute or two. He untethered her pony and let it into the niche. It stood patiently by the pile while he notched his arrow and spoke the requisite words. The string twanged, the shaft struck, the pony leapt and fell partly over the tomb. Those clear-cut things, happening rapidly, were out of tempo with everything else; they put a period to it.

CHAPTER TWENTY-ONE

I

Now began the four days of waiting. But just waiting was not enough; there had been no women to wail for her, no outcry of bereaved relatives; he would make it a vigil, all the four days should be one prayer. This was not an ordinary death.

It was quite dark, and the snow still drifted down like waterlogged leaves falling through water. He rebuilt the fire till it blazed, arranged the saddle-blanket and his saddle for a reclining place, pulled the trade blanket about him, and began the vigil, staring at the distant blacker place in the blackness of the cliffs behind the snowflakes that marked the niche.

He tried to pray, but his mind kept wandering, reviewing incidents of their life together, happy and unhappy, but so full of life, so charged with her personality. He would forget that she was dead, he would just be thinking about her. The cold coming through his clothing would wash along his skin, a flake would touch his face, and he would remember.

Now it is all over. Let it be altogether so. That horse is lucky; well, we shall go with her, too.

He got his pony, took his saddle in his hand, and went back into the niche. The animal was nervous and wild with the darkness and the cold and the smell of death. It would not stand still. Later it was to occur to him as part of the remarkableness that he went unhesitatingly into that place after dark, but now he thought nothing of it. Now he was not a Navajo terrified of the dead, not an Indian, not an individual of any race, but a man who had buried his own heart.

He selected his arrow.

'. . .It has not been in vain. You will remember me, I shall live in you.'

Wind God had spoken her words in his mind. She would not like this. He put back the arrow in his quiver, and led the horse out to the fire. There he took off its rope, and hobbled it.

'Go see if you can find food and water, little brother. Go away and be happy.'

He returned to his vigil, collecting a large pile of dead wood for the fire, and making himself as comfortable as possible with his blankets and his saddle. He began to feel some fear, conscious of the nearness of her tomb, being so very much alone in that narrow cañon. He set himself to the task of realizing what had happened, and conceiving a continuing life without Slim Girl. It was not easy; he spent a long time in rebellion, or in a mere thronging of bitter emotions that made him throw his shoulders from side to side.

Jesting Squaw's Son had been lucky. But in the end he was better off, because there had been that year and a half. Not for anything would he lose that. He began remembering again—it was a kind of anodyne— until he came back to the inevitable starting point. Then it was worse.

After some hours he grew calmer, partly because of fatigue. The disaster was accepted and familiar; he told himself that he could see the life ahead growing, in a way, from what had gone before. Nothing could ever make him forget; what he was and always would be, what he did and thought, would always be conditioned by Slim Girl. The remainder of his life would be a monument to her. All this could not be changed or taken from him, he would never lose its mark. That was a comfort.

He was thinking this way with his intellect, it did not really go inside of him. It was still just platitudes.

He became more aware of things about him, the cold, the fire, the snow. Flakes fell into the flames with little hisses, and he remembered his dream.

'Slayer of Enemy Gods' she called me. But Slayer of Enemy Gods spared the Cold Woman and Old Age Woman and Poverty People and Hunger People. She tried to kill the Hunger People; I thought she could. If we had not tried to do that, we should have been living happily within the Navajo country long ago. She was too daring, she wanted perfection.

By whatever means she got it, we had perfection. But it could not have gone on. We are not divine. Or I am not; she had made herself above Earth People. What has happened to me, it is like what happened to many people long ago. It happened to Taught Himself and the Magician's Daughter, to Reared in a Mountain when he went through the homes of the gods, to Eagles' Friend when he went to the sky. They went away and saw something better than they had ever known. They did not try to bring something too good for earth back to earth. But they did not—lose—Slim Girl.

His head fell forward on his knees and he stopped thinking. He was exhausted, and shortly fell asleep in that position. He woke when he began to fall over, very cold, and thought he must have drowsed. The fire was low. The snowfall ceased and dawn came limping.

The first day was sparkling, crisp, and sunny. The first day was one of stunned, dull realization. He wandered about uncertainly and drugged himself with detailed, long-drawn-out memories. And in the end, he would return to the beginning of his circle and stand or sit motionless and groan. It was a long day and a strange one; later he did not remember it clearly.

The second night he tried hard not to sleep, but it was hard, with cold, hunger, fatigue, and the fire. He dozed a good deal, and his memories became very accurate dreams into which slowly would creep a sense of horror without reason, until he woke, not knowing he had slept, continuing the thought and the mood. He tried to pray, but it was chiefly ejaculations and the names of the gods. It was an endless and terrible night.

Daylight, when at last it came, was a release. He shook himself, thinking, 'I must be calm, I must think clearly. This is no time for wandering without getting anywhere.' He quieted himself for a time, achieving a state of apparent resignation which enabled him to pray, but the oft-repeated *hozoji* sounded hollow. He did not really think there was anything beautiful; he was just acting as he thought he ought.

Plenty of people had died in his neighbourhood; there had been mourning and grief, when every one had stayed close to the hogahns for four days. But this was different. He had seen the bereaved, he had seen real sorrow upon them, but he could not believe that they had felt as he did.

He was alone in more than the physical sense. No one, not even Jesting Squaw's Son, could come near him. All his life, wherever he was, however long he lived, he would remain alone. It would always be like this. The one companionship in the world had gone; when the sun has been destroyed for a man, what comfort is there in a world of moonlight?

He had nothing to do in the cañon save tend his fire and think. He would get hold of a thought, work it over and over until he lost all sense of proportion towards it, and finally put it in a phrase or a simile, so that it obtained substance and could not be dismissed.

He hated to watch it grow dark; he felt afraid of the night. He did not want to be shut into that little space of firelight with all the things he was thinking. Alone, alone, all life alone, all life carrying this pain inside himself. He might as well die. But she wanted him to live. It was the third night, and he was approaching the stage of visions. Outlines of things dimly seen in the starlight changed and assumed startling forms. He became the audience listening to unseen people arguing as to whether he ought to kill himself or not. He knew he ought to live, but he could not control which side might win.

He couldn't always follow very well what was going on. Extraneous things intruded themselves. There were people all around, pitying him. It was being insisted upon that loneliness and pain were not worth enduring for a whole lifetime, without purpose.

'But I have to live for her,' he said aloud, and thought hard about her.

Then he saw her, standing on the other side of the fire. He started to his feet, choking with all a Navajo's terror of the walking dead. He was dissolved in fear, but she was gone. He was alone, the voices were gone, the people. He sat down, trembling, and quite wide awake. Evidently he did not want to die, but he had no will to live; he did not know himself, it would be wrong to make a decision now. Little by little he grew drowsy, and dozed in snatches. Perhaps her coming was a good thing; one would not expect her ghost to be like other people's.

This, too, became a discussion outside himself. The spirits of the dead are bad; if they walk, it is for destruction. She is different, she would come to protect him. She would lead him to some frightful end. But no one could imagine blue fire coming out of her eyes and mouth. It went on and on. There was an outline of something he had not seen before, it moved and he felt his scalp crawl. Then he let out a deep sigh and relaxed. It was a bush, some little distance away. Dawn was coming.

A little water and the clear sunshine revived him for a time, but soon he was tired and miserable again, listlessly occupying himself with gathering more firewood, bringing a branch at a time, setting aside without interest those that would do for making a sweat-bath. Later, he thought of that day as the day of treason. He protracted his occupation, being meticulous about finding all the wood in one section before moving to the next. He thought of the eventual bath, which should wash him clean of the taint of death; he wished it might wash out his mind. He thought that if he never had met her, he would be happy now, remembering Slender Hair riding by and telling him of the dance that was to be, remembering himself riding, singing, down to Tsé Lani, the firelight and that girl, remembering what chance, what meeting of eyes in a crowd, his uncle's tactlessness, had put an end to a young man who had no cares.

The thought stayed with him as he wandered about kicking up the snow for bits of dead wood. He knew that it was an entity in itself, and saw it as a tall old man who leered as he walked beside and slightly

184

behind him, a bad, strong old man. The old man kept at him about it, that he had been a fool, that he should have avoided all this. And he thought, in answer, that it was too late now, why couldn't he be left alone? He tried to explain to himself, to the old man, that he couldn't have helped doing what he did. He himself, as a third person, repeated that all the suffering was worth while for the happy months, but the old man only sneered. He tried to get himself in hand, and think of a new design for a belt, but that was useless. He would walk around for a long time without looking for wood at all. Picking up his pony's tracks, he followed them out into the main cañon until he saw the horse in a sheltered place under the east wall, then, realizing how far he had gone from the place of vigil, hurried back. Everything had gone to pieces, he did everything wrong. The old man had waited for him, he was triumphant over this breach of observance.

Nightfall was at least a change. Having plenty of wood, he built the fire up high, and went to some trouble to make himself comfortable. This was the fourth night, he was more or less out of his head. The old man had long ceased to be a personification and become a reality; he got in under the same blanket and hammered, hammered at him about the unfortunate past. Laughing Boy saw an empty, drifting future, always with this old man. He saw himself a long time from now, and the dead boy who had ridden down to Tsé Lani crying across a gap full of darkness to the empty husk of a man who had destroyed him. He tried to call on the gods, but there came only Hunger People, Old Age, and Cold Woman. Yellow Singer and his wife were there, looking sorry for him in that unpleasant, understanding way, like the day he was married. They all looked at him that way. He saw the stricken face of Jesting Squaw's Son, and thought, 'You too have received the wound, but you were lucky, the knife was pulled out as soon as it was thrust into you.'

The old man was pulling at his bow-guard. There was something around his right wrist, and that seemed to be being pulled too. The old man said,

'Where did you get that bow-guard?'

'I made it.'

'I'll give you six dollars for it.'

'I don't want to sell it.'

He did not really speak, but the words were saying themselves for him in answer to the old man, from a great distance, all the way from that hogahn by Tsé Lani.

The old man went on, 'That turquoise is no good, and the work is not very good.'

The work was good. He touched the silver with his right hand, to show the four-points-with-three-points design. But it was not that design, it was not the bow-guard he made at T'o Tlakai, it was that one he made at their hogahn, the one with stars-following.

He said out loud, 'This is the one I made when she was weaving. I will not sell it.'

He felt the thing on his right wrist; it was the thin, gold circlet. He saw her hand and arm under the blankets, he saw the tomb in the dusk, and her face as he bent over it, so still. His inturned torment was obliterated by the memory of that exalted agony. He remembered her last kiss, and her voice, and the mound of her blankets and jewels above her. His arms clutched about his knees, his left hand closed around the foreign bracelet, and he began to weep, tears pouring plenteously. As though they were rain on the desert, a coolness spread through him, a sense of majestic beauty.

He threw his arms wide, looked up, and began to pray,

> 'House made of dawn light,
> House made of evening light,
> House made of dark cloud,
> House made of he-rain . . .'

The old man was gone, and the Hunger People and all the rest. He stood up, stepping back from the fire, stretched out his hands, and his prayer rose in powerful song,

'Kat Yeinaezgani tla disitsaya . . .

'Now, Slayer of Enemy Gods, alone I see him coming,
Down from the skies, alone I see him coming.
His voice sounds all about,
His voice sounds, divine.
      Lé-é!
'Now, Child of the Waters, alone I see him coming . . .'

He finished, and stood with high head and hands
still held forth. A log on the fire fell in, the flames
leapt up, slightly dazzling his sight. When it had
cleared, along the level of his finger-tips he saw
a line dividing a deeper from a lesser blackness. The
line spread right and left, and now along its upper
edge a white glow appeared and widened; the sky
above was changing from black to blue, the cliffs
of the far side of the main cañon were silhouetted
against the coming day.
      'Hozoji, hozoji, hozoji, hozoji!

      'Dawn Boy, Little Chief,
      Let all be beautiful before me as I wander,
      All beautiful behind me as I wander,
      All beautiful above me as I wander,
      All beautiful below me as I wander.
      Let my eyes see only beauty
      This day as I wander.
      In beauty,
      In beauty,
      In beauty,
      In beauty!'

He let his arms fall. 'Thanks!'
He rearranged the fire to make a lasting, small
flame, enough to melt snow in the coffee-pot for
drinking and refreshing his hands and face. He looked
over towards the niche, a shadowy place; the rocks
on each side of it were touched irregularly with sunlight.
I nearly lost you, little sister, but now I have you
for always.
He began praying again, quietly and earnestly, not
in set terms, but according to his need. He had come
out of that closet in himself now, and things had fitted
back into place. He was grave, and there would be
many times when he would go by himself to feel
a belovéd pain, but regret for the knowledge of
187

happiness that had made that pain possible was ended. He had a clear conscience to pray.

He built his sweat-lodge, and, since it was hard to get mud out of the frozen ground, covered it with blankets. In the mid-afternoon he put in the hot rocks, stripped, and entered. He had made it good and hot; he sat in there chanting as long as he could stand it, then he burst out, rolled in the snow, and dressed hastily. He felt infinitely better. He looked at the sun, low in the west; the fourth day was ended.

He felt clear-headed, peaceful, washed, and very hungry as he tracked his pony. The animal greeted him with a whinny; its legs were stiff from the hobbles, and it had fallen off from lack of feed. He rode back to the camp, and tethered it while he broke his fast with coffee. Then he saddled and mounted. Before he rode on he turned towards the niche and sat still until his mount jerked at the reins.

But we shall never be far from each other, he thought, always alone but never lonely. As he rode away he repeated, 'In beauty it is finished, in beauty it is finished, in beauty it is finshed. Thanks.'

II

It was nearly dark when he climbed out of the head of the cañon onto the top of So Selah Mesa. He urged his pony along the level going, anxious to get to the settlement in Jaabani Valley as soon as possible. There was only a day-old moon, and a cold wind blew across the open. It was a talking wind, a voice of sorrow in the growing darkness, and Laughing Boy had been too long alone. He wanted a respite from self-communion; he wanted company and things happening, the old life, support. He was homesick for old, familiar things.

This cold plateau was nowhere, a waste land separating the human world from the enchanted. It was always dark here, and a cold wind blew, and there was always a small moon setting.

I shall be whimpering in a moment, he thought. I am unworthy of myself and of her. Do I forget everything? It's because I am cold and hungry. I might sing. He began,

'I rode down from high hills . . .'

but the high-pitched love-tune affronted the night. He stopped, with a catch in his throat.

I will not cry. This is not a thing to cry over; it is a beautiful thing, to be thought of gravely. I devote my life to it, not just cry. He began to chant, in a deep voice:

'With a place of hunger in me I wander,
    Food will not fill it,
    Aya-ah, beautiful.
With an empty place in me I wander,
    Nothing will fill it,
    Aya-ah, beautiful.
With a place of sorrow in me I wander,
    Time will not end it,
    Aya-ah, beautiful.
With a place of loneliness in me I wander,
    No one will fill it,
    Aya-ah, beautiful.
Forever alone, forever in sorrow I wander,
Forever empty, forever hungry I wander,
With the sorrow of great beauty I wander,
With the emptiness of great beauty I wander,
Never alone, never weeping, never empty,
Now on the old age trail, now on the path of beauty
    I wander,
    Ahalani, beautiful!'

It was a prayer. He ended with four solemn *hozoji's* that seemed to travel out from him and fill the darkness. That is a good song, he thought. I shall sing that often, at evening, when I am alone. But I wish we would get to where there are people.

It had been night for more than an hour when he came to the edge of the mesa, looking down into Jaabani. He saw the little pin-pricks of fires, very distant. Then, as he watched, near them another began, and grew, until a tall flame rose, throwing light all about it. He heard a drum beat and faint voices singing, and saw around the blaze a wide circle of branches, and people moving. They were beginning the last night of a Mountain Chant, the ritual within the Dark Circle of Branches.

'Come on, my pet!' His horse began slowly descending the trail in the starlight. As they went down, he sang his song again. This was very good. When Reared in a Mountain returned to his people from the homes of the gods, he taught them these prayers and songs, and they held the Mountain Chant for him, because he was unhappy among them. Even so was he. He was rejoining his people in the presence of the gods. Ah, if she could have been here!

The singing grew louder, the triumphant songs. Now he could make out the words. They were completing the magic of the tufted wands. He drew rein a few yards from one of the camp-fires, tasting again the sense of his isolation. Then he dismounted.

Only a few people remained outside the circle, but he found a hospitable pot of broth, some chunks of mutton still in it, bread to dip, and coffee.

'Where do you come from, Grandfather?' the woman asked.

'From Chiziai.'

'Where are you going?'

'To this dance.'

'That is a good saddle-blanket; who made it?'

'My wife, she weaves well.'

'Is she here?'

'No, she stayed behind.'

III

The brush fence enclosed an oval some forty feet across, in the centre of which blazed the bonfire, higher than a tall man. All around the edge sat people, several hundreds of them; they were happy, their faces were grave but joyful. At one end were the singers.

Now Red God came into the open space, leading a file of dancers, the Grandfather of the Gods, who guided Reared in a Mountain through the homes of the Divine Ones, who saved him from the Utes. With his plumed sticks and his sacred insignia, Red God led the dance before them.

190

Talking God and South God and Young Goddess came before them with dancers, and all the place was full of sacred songs. They were leading good dances, with good music.

The magicians came in and planted the yucca root. They sang and danced about it; the yucca grew, it became tall, it flowered. In midwinter the enchanted yucca bloomed before them. These were the magics that the people of distant tribes brought to the first Mountain Chant. Now the magicians placed the board and the disk of the sun on the ground, the people all shouted, 'Stand! Stand!' The board stood up on end, the sun rose to the top and set slowly; four times the sun rose and set by magic; then the board lay flat again.

A man, stripped to his breech-clout, danced before a basket. Out of the basket an eagle feather rose; it danced up into the air, to the height of the man, and there it moved backward and forward in time with him.

Jesters came in, dressed as Americans and Mexicans, and made the people laugh. The spirits of the ancestral animals, hovering over the brush circle, were made happy. Laughing Boy, sitting among friendly strangers, smiled at them and said,

'It is good!'

The great central fire and the small fires that people made for themselves, kept the place warm. He had eaten, he was comfortable. He did not realize how sleepy he was. At times the details of what he was watching became blurred and he drowsed deliciously; but he was permeated with the general feeling of the prayer, and he looked upon it as he had when an uninitiated child.

Young men painted all white with black forearms, foxskins hanging from their waists, came in with the magic arrows adorned with breath-feathers. This was the holiest part; this was the charm that the Tall Gods taught to Reared in a Mountain in their divine home. The young men danced, they swallowed the arrows and shouted in triumph; these were the very acts of the gods.

Laughing Boy felt a deep sense of peace, and rejoicing over ugliness defeated. The gods danced before him, he felt the influence of their divinity.

The naked youths danced with torches, they bathed in flame, they leapt through and through the fire. He had been bathed in flame, he had been through a fire.

The past and the present came together, he was one with himself. The good and true things he had thought entered into his being and were part of the whole continuity of his life.

It was beginning to dawn, the last prayer came to a close. Quietly, the people left the enclosure. He went to where his horse was tethered and rolled up in his blanket. Sleepily there, he kissed the gold bracelet, saying,

'Never alone, never lamenting, never empty, *Ahalani,* beautiful!'